D1295808

BOUNTY MAN

Also available in Large Print
by Lewis B. Patten:

Ambush at Soda Creek
The Cheyenne Pool
Death Rides a Black Horse
The Law in Cottonwood
Man Outgunned
Ride a Tall Horse
Showdown at Mesilla
The Trail of the Apache Kid

BOUNTY MAN

Lewis B. Patten

G.K.HALL &CO.
Boston, Massachusetts
1984
MAY 2 4 1984

Copyright © 1974 by Lewis B. Patten

All Rights Reserved

All of the characters in this book are fictitious, and any resemblance to actual persons, living or dead, is purely coincidental.

Published in Large Print by arrangement with Doubleday & Company, Inc.

Set in 18 pt English Times

Library of Congress Cataloging in Publication Data

Patten, Lewis B.
  Bounty man.

  "Published in large print"—Verso t.p.
  1. Large type books. I. Title.
[PS3566.A79B6 1984]   813'.54   83-22838
ISBN 0-8161-3623-8

BOUNTY MAN

Chapter 1

A single road from the outside world served the town of Dry Creek, but it dead-ended there. Which is not to say no other roads left the ugly little town. Two did, one running like a snake due north across adobe flats covered with head-high greasewood and little else. It continued for thirty miles, getting smaller and narrower with each rundown ranch or shack it passed, until finally it just petered out in some high grass near the head of a dry, deep gulch that had no name, at least none that were not profane. This same gulch carried a wall of water down the valley every time it rained heavily, so that no one even tried to bridge the gully any more. The road descended into it and climbed back out at least fifty times in its thirty miles of length.

The other road went west, into a maze of rounded, cedar-covered hills, each of which looked almost exactly like the last so that anyone except a native could easily get lost, at least if he strayed very far from the road. Like the other, this road finally just petered out.

Into this country and into this town rode Ross Dunbar on the 21st day of July in 1881. He was a tall and lanky man of thirty-five, dried out by the sun and brown as the cracked saddle beneath his bony rump. His hat was shapeless from repeated wettings and stained with sweat and dust, and there was a hole in the crown in front and a matching one in back, which might have been made by a bullet except that since Dunbar talked so little about himself it wasn't likely anyone would ever find out from him.

He wore a blue work shirt, faded and stained with sweat, gray woolen pants and high-topped Texas boots that might have been either black or brown when they were new a long, long time ago. Now they were scuffed and run down at the heel, and on the side of the right one was a hole through

which Dunbar's bare foot was visible.
Behind his saddle was a slicker-wrapped
bundle holding a pair of scuffed chaps, a
blanket, a sack of grub and a few blackened
cooking utensils because Dunbar ate more
meals in the open than he ever did within
four walls. A saddle scabbard held a rifle,
the stock of which was scratched and worn,
and there was a beat-up gun belt around his
waist filled with corroded greenish cartridges
for his revolver. An old cavalry canteen hung
by its strap from the saddle horn.

The revolver itself was as scuffed as the
rifle. It had walnut grips, one of which was
cracked. What metal showed was rusty, yet
there was something about this man that
made you believe his guns would shoot
where he pointed them despite their dis-
repair. Behind his saddle were a pair of
cracked saddlebags that held his personal
possessions, a clean, if rumpled shirt, socks
and underwear, a razor and strop, a cake of
shaving soap, a few loose pieces of brown
jerky that didn't even look edible, some
papers and a sack of loose gold coins.

Hat pulled low over his eyes against the
slanting rays of the late afternoon sun, he
bypassed the bridge just short of town, let
his horse drink from the nearly dry creek

which gave the town its name, then climbed out on the other side. He headed up the dusty street.

He stared about with distaste. This town was similar to a hundred others he had visited, but he always kept hoping one would be different, a clean town with white houses and white picket fences and bushes with lilacs on them and little bright flower gardens in front. Here there wasn't even a blade of grass and there were damn few trees.

He rode in the exact center of the street. His horse plodded a little faster than before knowing that town meant hay and sometimes a little grain.

Dunbar kept his eyes straight ahead, even though the feeling of being watched was almost physical. He told himself that the interest everybody took in him was because of the fact that no one came here unless they lived or had business here. Even so, their steady regard made him edgy. He felt the way he'd sometimes felt riding through Indian country, knowing that hostile eyes followed his every move.

Close to the bridge there were several shacks that looked uninhabited. Next there was a livery stable that leaned at least two feet off square. It looked as if a good wind

4

would blow it down. A ramp led up into it from the street and the horse took the ramp gingerly, as if afraid he would break through.

The liveryman, like everybody else in town, had been watching him. He stood at one side of the door as Dunbar swung stiffly down. Dunbar got his saddlebags from behind the saddle, slung them over a shoulder, then said, "Hay and a little oats, but not too much. Rubdown wouldn't hurt."

The liveryman was short and scrawny like an apple dried up by the sun. He had an Adam's apple that bobbed up and down when he swallowed and he hadn't shaved for several days. A sour smell emanated from him that had nothing to do with the stable, being simply an unwashed smell. Dunbar supposed he smelled as bad himself. The man said scratchily, "Stayin' long?"

Dunbar stared at him and the liveryman looked away. Without bothering to reply, Dunbar went down the ramp into the street and turned uptown.

The upper end wasn't much better than the lower except that it looked inhabited. There was a store whose roof at midday shaded the boardwalk and a bench. There was a saloon, its swinging doors tied back to let in all the air possible. There was a big, two-story building that looked more like a house than a hotel, but a weathered sign over the door proclaimed that it was a hotel. Apparently it didn't have a name.

Dunbar thought the whole place looked like it had been sandblasted. There was hardly any paint left on anything, and most of the signs were all but unreadable. Nowhere did he see a jail or lawman's office. The town was probably too small to afford any law. Maybe they didn't need any, or maybe they just made their own as they went along, settling what quarrels they had by themselves.

He walked up the street to the hotel and he seemed to feel hostility in the townspeople's stares. He stepped up the three steps to the hotel doorway and went in.

There was a small lobby, its floor bare wood, furnished with seedy-looking couches and chairs. In one corner was the desk and behind it was a pimply-faced youth of about sixteen. He was trying to grow a mustache, but it was a forlorn attempt. He looked at Dunbar almost guiltily. "Yes, sir?"

"Room. On the street."

"Yes, sir." The youth shoved a dog-eared register across the counter toward him.

6

Dunbar signed his name. The youth looked at it, then asked nervously, "Will you be staying long?"

Everybody seemed to be worrying about how long he'd be staying, Dunbar thought. He said, "The key, son. The key."

The boy got the key from a cubbyhole. He dropped it, picked it up, and then shoved it across the desk. Dunbar picked it up, turned, and climbed the stairs. He noticed that the third, seventh, and ninth steps creaked. So did the hallway, at almost every step.

He found his room and unlocked the door. He went in and closed it behind him. The room was hot and airless. Several flies droned against the window behind the windowshade.

Dunbar dropped his saddlebags on the bed, crossed the room and raised the shade. He opened the window but there wasn't any breeze. The temperature in the room must be 95 at least, he thought, and it wouldn't get much cooler until the sun went down.

Staring into the street at the ugly buildings and bleak landscape beyond, he wondered why he had been foolish enough to come.

Dunbar had no more than disappeared into the hotel before Mitch Harrow headed for

7

the livery barn. Mitch had a place north of town about ten miles. He had come in this morning after a few supplies, coffee, sugar, and stock salt.

He was a man with the look of defeat to him. It showed in the straggly growth of whiskers he had not even bothered to shave for this rare trip to town. It showed in his clothes, dirty and bad-smelling. It showed in his slouch and the way he stooped as if life's burdens were too great for him to bear.

Forty-five, he was, and his seamed face was worried as he walked up the ramp toward Ray Fleming, the liveryman. "Who is he?" he asked.

Fleming shrugged. "Didn't say."

"How long's he goin' to stay?"

"Didn't say that neither."

"Why the hell would he want to come to this goddam town?"

"You came, didn't you?"

"Wish to God I hadn't."

The liveryman looked slyly at him. "You can leave, any time you're a mind."

Harrow scowled and did not reply. He looked around until he spotted Dunbar's saddle on the plank floor of the livery barn.

"Yep."

Harrow walked over to it. Fleming said,

"You leave it be. I ain't goin' to have him on my back because somebody got into his gear."

Harrow looked longingly at the rolled-up gear tied behind the saddle. He said, "Might be somethin' in there that would tell us who he was."

"Go on up to the hotel an' look at the register."

Harrow nodded. He stared at the saddle a moment more, then went out into the late-afternoon sun. He slouched up the street toward the hotel. Short of it by fifty yards, he raised his glance to the second story. The stranger was standing in one of the windows looking down. For the briefest instant their glances met. Harrow quickly looked away.

He went into the hotel, feeling something cold in his gut, like ice. He crossed the lobby floor to the desk. Delbert Franks, the youthful clerk, glanced up at him. "Hello, Mr. Harrow."

Harrow nodded. "What name did he sign?"

"Who?" Franks asked.

Harrow said disgustedly, "Now who the hell do you think? How many strangers have signed that register today?"

Franks looked at the register. He squinted,

trying to read Dunbar's scrawl. "Looks like Dunbar. Ross Dunbar."

The name meant nothing to Harrow. He nodded and went back outside. It was hot and still, but he was used to it. He walked back down to the livery barn. "Name's Dunbar," he said. "Ross Dunbar. Mean anything to you?"

Fleming shook his head.

Harrow said, "He ain't going to be coming back here tonight. Let's look in his blanket roll."

Fleming glanced up toward the hotel uneasily. Finally he said grudgingly, "Well, all right. But I'll stay here an' watch. If he starts this way, I'll let you know."

Harrow walked to the saddle. He knelt and untied the saddle strings. He laid the slicker-wrapped bundle on the floor and unrolled it carefully. Inside the slicker there was a pair of scuffed chaps. Rolled up in them was a blanket, a sack of grub and a gunny sack with some blackened cooking utensils in it. And there was something else, a roll of papers tied with a piece of string.

Harrow didn't have to unroll them to know what they were. Reward posters, a lot of them. He said, "The son-of-a-bitch is a bounty hunter. That's what he is."

Fleming left the doorway and came to where Harrow was. He said, "Jesus! I wonder who he's after here."

Harrow's hand was shaking as he replaced the papers and began to roll up the bundle the way it had been before. Fleming asked, "Hadn't we ought to look at them?"

Harrow didn't glance up at him. He growled, "Why? Is your face on one of 'em?"

"No, by God, it ain't. But I'll bet yours is. Else why'd you want to snoop in the man's bedroll?"

Harrow finished with the bedroll and retied it behind Dunbar's saddle. He got out as quickly as he could. He thought, Damn! God damn him to hell! How'd he ever find me here?

Chapter 2

Mitch Harrow went into the saloon. He seldom drank because he had little money for it, but this afternoon he felt as if he had to have a drink. Seeing that roll of bounty posters in Dunbar's bedroll had given him a shock. He wished now that he hadn't let it shake him up so badly. He wished he'd opened the roll and gone through it to see if a poster on him was really there. But he hadn't wanted Fleming to see it if there was.

Maybe it wasn't, he told himself. It had been a long time. Maybe they'd given up. But if they had, why was this bounty hunter here?

He went to the bar, hauled out a soiled

bandanna and wiped his face. The saloon-keeper, Jake Montoya, looked at him expectantly. Mitch said, "Whiskey."

Montoya nodded. He brought bottle and glass and poured out a couple of fingers for Mitch. He said, "Hot."

Harrow nodded. He wiped his face again. He put the bandanna away and picked up the glass. His hand shook so badly that even the small amount of whiskey in the glass almost spilled. He noticed that Montoya was watching his hand. He gulped the whiskey and dropped his hand below the level of the bar. He didn't look at Montoya and after a moment Montoya left and walked down to the other end of the bar where he had a stool.

Harrow poured himself another drink. He gulped it too, glancing at Montoya to see if he was watching. Montoya was.

Harrow got up and crossed the room. He looked across the street at the hotel. One upstairs window was open, this being the one in which he had seen the newcomer, Ross Dunbar. It was empty now.

He went back to the bar, poured and gulped another drink. He fished a quarter out of the leather pocketbook he carried and placed it on the bar. He looked at Montoya.

"Three for a quarter. Right?"

"That's right."

Harrow turned and walked to the door. He wished he could sneak out the back but he knew that would look funny to Montoya and might be mentioned later.

He thought about the roll of bounty posters in the stranger's bedroll, and he suddenly knew he'd never have any peace again until he had looked at each of them. He left the saloon and walked down the street toward the livery barn without glancing at the hotel. But he didn't go in the front. He skirted the side and went to the back. Out here there was a big corral with about a dozen horses in it. On one side several rigs were parked. He wondered where Fleming was. Usually at this time of the day the stableman went up to the saloon for a beer. He'd have to wait until Fleming left.

He eased the corral gate open, wincing when it squeaked. He went through and barred the gate behind him. He eased along the wall to the back door.

He could see clear through the barn from back to front. Fleming was sitting on a box just inside the big front door, looking out.

Harrow waited. His knees shook so badly that he pressed them against the stable wall to make them stop. Fleming was puffing on a pipe.

Harrow thought, Damn you, go on! You always go for a beer this time of day!

But Fleming didn't move. Harrow fidgeted. Half an hour passed. Finally Fleming got up, knocked out his pipe on the heel of his hand and put it away. He stretched, then walked out the door, down the ramp and into the street.

Harrow went in hurriedly. Nearly running, he went to the front door, staying in the powdered manure so that Fleming wouldn't hear his footsteps on the floor. He reached the front door and peered out. Fleming was already half a block away.

Harrow glanced at the hotel. There was no sign of the stranger. No one else was closer to the stable than half a block.

Quickly he turned and went to Dunbar's saddle. With trembling fingers he untied the saddle strings. He hurried back to the door and peered out again. Seeing nothing, he returned.

He unrolled the blanket roll quickly and took the string-tied bundle of papers out. He laid it aside, rerolled the blanket roll in the slicker and tied it on behind the saddle again. He looked up toward the door, starting violently at seeing movement there. But it was only Fleming's black dog, wagging his tail and looking curiously at him.

Harrow was, by now, bathed with sweat. He glanced at Dunbar's saddle to see if the blanket roll looked the same. He decided it looked good enough. It didn't really matter anyway. As soon as Dunbar opened it he'd know it had been tampered with.

The dog turned his head and looked at something in the direction of the hotel. Harrow grabbed up the roll of papers and ran. He reached the back door and burst out into the corral so suddenly that he startled the horses. They plunged away from him and began circling the corral at a run.

Damn, he thought, and plunged out through the gate, not worrying now about the squeak. He stuffed the papers inside his shirt and headed down the alley toward the edge of town. Just before he came to the bed of the creek, he looked back. No one was following or even watching him.

Out of sight in the creek bottom he scurried along until he was about a quarter mile from town. Then he sat down, put his back to a stunted tree and took the bundle out.

He was sweating and out of breath, but he

was also cold. Maybe if he destroyed these wanted posters, Dunbar would go away. He wouldn't have anything to go on. By the time the bounty hunter left, replaced the posters and came back, he himself could be a long ways from here.

He thumbed through them quickly, looking for the name he'd used to go by or for a picture of himself. He didn't find it, but he found something else. He found Quirino Madrid's picture. There was a $500 reward and the charge was murder.

He also found a poster on Grady Morse, wanted by Wells Fargo for stagecoach robbery and murder along with another man, whose picture was not shown, but who, Harrow decided, might be Ed Huett, who had arrived here with Morse a year ago. The reward for them was $750 each.

He finished going through the wanted posters. He realized that his hands had stopped shaking and that he wasn't sweating any more. There was no poster on him here. Apparently the bounty hunter wasn't after him.

Suddenly his stomach began jumping again. Maybe the bounty hunter had other posters on his person or in his saddle-bags. All of them might not have been in his blanket roll.

He rolled up the posters and retied them. He got up and stuffed the roll back into his shirt. The first thing he should do was see Grady Morse and Quirino Madrid. He'd show them the posters and let them take it from there. They'd kill the bounty hunter and dispose of his body and that would be the end of it. He wouldn't have to do anything himself.

Feeling much relieved now that he had decided upon a course, he headed back toward town.

The first thing Dunbar did when he turned away from the window was to lie down on the bed. He stared gloomily at the cracked and peeling ceiling. The flies still droned against the window. The air was hot and nearly motionless. He could feel sweat springing from his pores.

He was tired, but he knew he couldn't sleep. Not until evening when it cooled off. He got up, took off his shirt and the upper half of his underwear. He poured water into the washbasin and washed from the waist on up. He wet his hair and face, then got the razor and soap from his saddlebags. He stropped the razor, lathered his face and shaved. With a piece of broken comb, he combed his hair. He wished he could change underwear but he wanted to save his clean underwear and shirt for tomorrow.

He dried himself on the towel, which looked as if it hadn't been changed after the last occupant checked out, then replaced the upper half of his underwear and his shirt. Putting on his hat, he headed for the door. He took his saddlebags with him. Carrying them would attract attention but he didn't want to leave them in the room, even if the door was locked.

The youthful clerk stared at him but when he glanced at the boy, the clerk quickly looked away. Carrying his saddlebags, Dunbar went outside.

For several moments he stood on the sidewalk, looking up the street and down. Once more he felt watched. He crossed to the saloon.

There was a dark-skinned man behind the bar, part Mexican, Dunbar thought. He looked amiable. Dunbar walked to the bar, laid down his saddlebags and said, "Beer."

The man drew a schooner. He brought it to Dunbar and put it down in front of him. He said, "That'll be a nickel."

Dunbar put a nickel down. He tasted the

beer which, surprisingly, was cool. The bartender didn't say anything so finally Dunbar said, "What keeps people alive in a place like this? Do they raise cattle, or sheep, or what?"

The bartender apparently wasn't as amiable as he looked. He said sourly, "If you don't like it, you don't have to stay."

"Don't intend to," Dunbar said. "You can tell that to the rest of them and maybe they'll quit watching me."

"We don't get many strangers here. Ain't no train. The most excitement we get is when the mud wagon comes in twice a month with mail. Can't blame 'em for wonderin' what a man would be comin' here for. Road dead-ends. Ain't nothing on beyond."

Dunbar didn't say anything.

The bartender said, "You lookin' for somebody?"

Dunbar took a gulp of beer and wiped his mouth with the back of his hand.

The bartender said irritably, "All right. Don't talk. Ain't no skin off my nose."

Dunbar shrugged. He could have told the man who he was looking for and asked directions but he wanted to keep it private if he could. He'd eventually have to ask somebody, but not a talky bartender who would have it all over town in an hour or two.

He finished his beer. "Where's the best place to eat?"

"Hotel. Cookin's done by Ma O'Rourke. Tonight it's stew."

Dunbar finished the beer and ordered another one. He put another nickel down. He was beginning to wonder at himself for coming here and he dreaded what lay ahead. But he'd come this far and would not now go back.

He took his time with the second beer. Three other men came in, stared until he caught their glances, then quickly looked away. After that he could feel them watching him.

He supposed it was natural enough to stare at a stranger in a town this isolated and to wonder what he was doing here. But that didn't make him like it any more.

The beer finished, he left and crossed the street to the hotel. The sun was low in the west and cast long shadows across the street. The air, surprisingly, was cooler and there was a little breeze stirring that made it feel cooler than it really was.

He dreaded going into the stuffy, hot hotel. Delaying it, he sat down on one of the

21

hotel steps. He stared at the bleak and ugly town. The life he led had been bothering him more and more of late and it bothered him tonight.

He lived too much alone. He had no family and no friends. He didn't even have a dog. Sometimes it got so damn bad he got to talking to himself. And sometimes he was so lonely for a woman it was almost a hurt. Saloon and bawdy-house girls stopped it from bothering him for a while but never made it completely go away.

He wanted more from a woman than bawdy-house girls were prepared to give. Or maybe he never gave them a chance to give him more than he paid them for.

Other times, when he'd see children playing in a street and hear their shrill shouts, a different kind of ache would come to him.

He ought to quit, he thought. The loss that had made him begin was six years past and it was time he stopped letting it twist and control his life.

He had money put away. He could buy a ranch someplace and stock it. He'd be no more alone than he was now. Maybe it *was* blood money but money was money and likely it all had some blood on it.

Besides that, he felt no guilt over what he had been doing the past six years. He was just doing a job the law either couldn't or wouldn't do.

Chapter 3

Harrow rode out of town a little before sundown. Dunbar was sitting on the steps of the hotel. He did not look at Harrow and, after that first quick glance, Harrow didn't look at him.

It didn't surprise him that Morse, Huett, and Madrid were also fugitives. They had probably blundered into this dead-end place just the way he had. It had looked like a good place to hide and it had been, at least until now. There was no law closer than the county seat, fifty miles away. The sheriff never came here unless he had to. That wasn't more than a couple of times a year and he didn't poke around when he came.

He just took care of his business and went home.

Now Harrow began to wonder how many more of Dry Creek's residents were running from the law. Hell, maybe a lot of them. Why else would anyone stay in this God-forsaken place? It took fifty acres to feed a sheep. It took a hundred and fifty to feed a cow, and nothing that came from here ever went to market fat.

If it wasn't for the deer over in the cedar breaks a man would starve to death. Harrow himself lived almost exclusively on venison. What few cattle he sold made the payments on his ranch, if you could call it that, and provided staples like sugar, coffee, and salt. He raised a few vegetables and always put in a quarter acre of spuds from which he harvested a couple of hundred pounds not much bigger than walnuts.

It was dusk when he rode past Daisy Elbert's place. It looked bleak and barren, but there was a lamp shining from one of the windows, and he could see young Luke driving the milch cow in. Faintly he could hear the cow's bell tinkling.

He went on up the road, thinking about Daisy. Like every other single man in the valley, he'd tried to make friends with her.

He hadn't succeeded any better than the others and he'd finally given up. She was a pretty woman, but a man just wasted his time with her. She had a husband someplace, a fact she never let a man forget.

He wondered why Daisy stayed in a place where living was as hard as it was here. He had a reason and so did Morse and Madrid. But what about her? Why was she satisfied to scratch out a starvation living when all she had to do to escape it was get on a horse and ride away? And why didn't her husband send for her? Unless he was in prison.

He shrugged, tiring quickly of thinking about something as puzzling as the actions of his fellow humans. He went on up the road until he saw the light that marked the small log cabin of Quirino Madrid. Madrid ran sheep, more than anyone else hereabouts. He was a Mexican and he understood sheep because his family had run sheep for hundreds of years in Mexico. Harrow wondered briefly who Madrid had killed and why.

He opened the gate and rode down the long lane toward the cabin. While he still was a hundred yards away, he called, "Madrid? It's Mitch! Mitch Harrow!" If a man was wanted for murder it wasn't a good idea to ride in on him unannounced.

The door opened and Madrid stood framed in it. He didn't ask Harrow to dismount. He didn't like Harrow and had never tried to pretend otherwise.

Harrow said, "I come to do you a favor."

Madrid waited.

Harrow said. "There's a stranger in Dry Creek. Name's Dunbar. Bounty man."

For several moments Madrid stood there motionless. Harrow couldn't see his face because the light was in back of him. But he could sense the tension in the Mexican. Harrow, a little irritated because of the coolness of his reception, said bluntly, "He's got a poster on you, Madrid. Charge is murder and the reward is five hundred dollars."

Madrid said, "Get down and come in. There's coffee or wine if you prefer."

"Don't mind if I do." Harrow slid to the ground. He walked to the door and Madrid stood aside. Madrid said, "It was a long time ago. I thought they had forgotten it."

"Must've been somebody who didn't want to forget."

Madrid nodded. He got a wine bottle and poured some in a tin cup for Mitch. He poured some into another cup for himself.

He said, "Why did you come? You could have shared the reward if you had turned me in."

"Money ain't everything. A man don't turn in his friends."

"I am not your friend and you know I'm not."

Harrow felt his face getting hot. He could feel an irritable anger rising in him. He'd had the hell scared out of him today. It was hot and he was still scared and now he was getting trouble from Madrid. He gulped the wine and got to his feet. "All right. To hell with you. I just thought . . ."

Madrid said, "You're wanted too, aren't you? It's the only possible reason you would not have turned me in."

"I am like hell!" Harrow blustered. "I . . ." But it wasn't any good. He could see that it was not. Madrid knew. And if Madrid was caught he might give the secret away, accidentally or intentionally. What he ought to do, he thought, was kill Madrid and turn him over to the bounty man. Get the reward before . . . But it wouldn't work. Getting bounty money sometimes took two or three weeks. During that time he'd still be here under the eye of the bounty man. If the man did have a poster on him, he'd be sure to find it and match it up with him.

Madrid saw the thought in his eyes and saw it go away. He said, "I thank you for telling me."

"What are you goin' to do?"

"Nothing."

"You ain't going to run?"

Madrid shook his head.

"And you ain't going to kill the man?"

"I have killed once. That's enough."

Harrow could see he wasn't going to get far here. He nodded sourly and went out into the night. He mounted, wishing he had another drink of that wine but unwilling to ask for it.

He reached the road and turned north again. Morse and Huett lived in a little adobe shack about fifteen miles from town. It was beyond his own place by a couple of miles.

He didn't stop at his own place, but rode on up the road. It was strange when he thought of it now that he hadn't suspected Morse and Huett before. They had no cattle and they had no sheep. They raised no crops. They didn't work for anybody else. They had no visible means of support.

They sometimes disappeared for a month or so and then came back claiming they'd had work over in Utah, or up in Wyoming, or someplace else. It had occurred to Harrow once that maybe they hired out their guns, but he hadn't dwelt on the possibility long because he was too preoccupied with his own affairs.

A light glowed dimly from a window of the adobe shack. Once more, as he approached, Harrow called out so that he wouldn't come on them by surprise. The door opened, and Morse stood framed in it, a rifle in his hands. Harrow called, "It's me, Mitch Harrow."

Morse leaned the rifle against the wall. "What're you doin' away up here?"

Harrow got down without being asked. He went to the door. "Mind if I come in?"

Morse stood aside. Harrow went in. The place had a packed earth floor. There were bunks at the far end, rumpled and unmade, and a table in the center. There was a sheet-iron stove for cooking and a stand with a bucket of water, a dipper, and a washpan on it. A lamp was on the table, a bottle of whiskey beside it. Harrow stared at it until Huett said, "I take it you want a drink."

"Don't mind if I do." Harrow accepted a tin cup half filled with the amber liquid. He took a gulp, then said, "There's a bounty man in town. He's got a poster on you."

Neither man showed surprise. Morse asked, "On who? Me or Ed?"

"On you. Your picture is on it. It says there's another man wanted, but there ain't no picture of him. I figured it might be Ed."

"How'd *you* come to see it?"

Harrow hadn't prepared himself for this question and for several moments he groped frantically for some plausible reply. Morse suddenly grabbed him by the shirt front and yanked him close. "How? Tell me, you little weasel, before I break you in two!"

Harrow broke out in a cold sweat. He should have stayed away from here, he thought. He should have stayed out of it. He could have gone back into the cedars for a couple of weeks. By the time he came back, the bounty hunter would probably have been gone. But he hadn't, and now it was too late.

He said, "He looked . . . well, I couldn't figure why anybody would come to Dry Creek so I went through his blanket roll." He reached into his shirt and pulled out the roll of posters. "I found these. I went through them and found the ones on you and Madrid."

Morse released him and broke the string

on the posters. He spread them out on the table and went quickly through them. He found the one on himself and the one on Quirino Madrid. Holding the two, he looked at Mitch. "Where's the one on you? Did you tear it up?"

"There wasn't one. I ain't . . ." He didn't get to finish. Morse's hard, bony fist smashed his mouth and sent him against the stove. He put out his hands to save himself and they touched down, flat, on the hot surface of the stove.

He uttered a sound of pain very near a shriek. He sank to the floor, staring at his hands. They were seared like a piece of meat.

Morse repeated callously, "Where's the one on you?"

Harrow knew it would do him no good to keep on denying that there had been a poster on him in the roll. Morse would continue beating him. He said, "I burned it."

"That's better. What're *you* wanted for? Stealin' eggs from a chickenhouse?"

Something made Mitch feel compelled to defend himself. He said, "Murder. I'm wanted for murder."

"Well I'll be damned! What do you think of that, Ed? The little rooster says he killed someone."

Mitch started to get up. His hands pained him excruciatingly. Morse asked, "Who'd you kill?"

"I . . ."

Morse kicked him. Involuntarily Harrow put out his hands to check his fall and when they touched the floor he cried out again with pain. Morse said, "Who?"

"My wife. I caught her with another man."

Morse laughed wickedly. "I thought it must have been a woman. You wouldn't have the sand it takes to kill another man."

Harrow was beginning to get scared. He hadn't expected them to treat him this way. He'd done them a favor and he'd expected them to appreciate what he'd done. Instead, they were abusing him.

He struggled to his feet. "I got to get on home and look after these hands. I burned them pretty bad."

Morse said, with mock pity, "Too bad. But they ain't going to hurt you long."

"What do you mean? I done you a favor. If I hadn't warned you . . ."

Morse said, "You're the only one that can put that poster together with the two of us."

"But I won't! I swear I won't! Hell, I'm wanted too. I'd be cuttin' my own damn throat . . ."

There was a gun in Morse's hand. He said, "Ed, go get a couple of horses saddled up."

Harrow turned to run. They were going to murder him. He beat Ed Huett to the door and plunged through it.

The bullet took him in the back, shattering his spine. There was no pain, only an eerie floating sensation that lasted but an instant or two.

Morse holstered the smoking gun. Huett went out, stepping over Harrow's body. He disappeared into the darkness.

Morse got a couple of gunny sacks. He laid them on the ground beside Harrow and rolled him into them so that he wouldn't bleed all over the ground outside the door. There was already a small spot of blood. He scratched at it with a boot toe until he had scattered it.

He went back into the house. He kept out the poster with Quirino Madrid's picture on it and threw the rest into the stove. The bounty hunter might suspect there were wanted men in Dry Creek when he discovered that his blanket roll had been rifled, but without the posters he wouldn't know who. He might eventually get duplicates, but that would take time. Time enough for the two of them to get away.

Then Morse shook his head. For a year now, this had been a good place to hide. They'd been able to make forays away from here, to pull a robbery or to enjoy the bright lights in Denver or Cheyenne. If they let this bounty hunter get away, they'd have to leave themselves.

Huett came back with the horses. Together they loaded Harrow and tied him down. Then they mounted and rode into the darkness, westward into the maze of cedar hills.

Chapter 4

Ross Dunbar awoke when first light grayed the sky. He got up, went to the window and stared down into the street. He ran his fingers through his hair, yawned and scratched his belly industriously.

Having done that, he crossed the room to the dresser and poured water from the china pitcher into the cracked china basin. He washed his face, then stripped off his underwear and took a spit bath in the water that was left. He got his clean suit of underwear out of the saddlebags and put it on. He put on his pants and boots, shaved, then put on his clean shirt. By the time he had finished, the sun was poking its rim above the horizon in the east.

Dunbar stuffed his dirty clothes into the saddlebags, slung them over a shoulder and went downstairs. There was nobody at the desk. He could smell coffee though, so he knew Ma O'Rourke was in the hotel kitchen.

He went outside and stood for a moment on the hotel steps. The air was cool and fresh. The sun upon the sagebrush had given the air a pungent smell that was in no way unpleasant. He stood there soaking up the sun a moment, then turned and went into the hotel dining room.

He put the saddlebags and his hat on one chair and sat down in another. Apparently he had not been heard. He got up and went to the kitchen door. He poked in his head and said, "Mornin'."

Ma O'Rourke whirled, startled. She said, "You startled me."

"Sorry. Can I have something to eat?"

"Sure. Just go sit down and I'll bring yer coffee in to you."

Dunbar went back to his table and sat down. A moment later, Mrs. O'Rourke brought him a pot of coffee and a cup. She poured it for him, watching him so steadily that she spilled the coffee. Dunbar grinned wryly as, flustered, she wiped it up with her apron and hurried away.

He sipped the coffee appreciatively. It didn't look as if he was going to find out what he had to know without asking, so when Mrs. O'Rourke came back with a plate of fried ham, scrambled eggs, and fried potatoes, he asked, "Where's the Elbert place?"

"Daisy Elbert's place?"

He said, "Frank Elbert's place."

"Ain't but one family of Elberts hereabouts. That's Daisy an' her boy. Place is up north on that road that follows the dry wash. Let's see . . . I think it's the third house, maybe five, six miles from town."

He said, "Thank you ma'am."

"What you want Daisy fer?"

He stared straight at her without answering. Moving away, she grumbled, "All right, all right. So it ain't none of me damn business. You don't have to be so blasted uppity."

He finished his meal and left a quarter on the table. He got up, picked up his saddlebags and put on his hat. He went out and walked down the street to the stable. Once more he felt as if he was being watched, and once, as he glanced up, he saw a curtain in an upstairs window stir.

The stableman was nowhere around. Dunbar went back along the passageway until he found his horse standing in a stall. He led him out.

He knew the instant he saw his saddle that the blanket roll had been tampered with. He untied the saddle strings and unrolled the bundle. The bounty posters were gone.

He rolled it up again and retied it behind his saddle, then threw the saddle on and cinched it down. He bridled the horse, mounted and rode out into the street. But he did not go north. He went back the way he had come, turning when he came to the creek and circling along its course until he could climb out and cut across country toward the road heading north without being seen.

There could be only one explanation for the missing posters. Someone in Dry Creek had a bounty on his head. His picture might have been among those he had been carrying. Or it might not. There could, in fact, be several wanted men living here. It was an ideal spot to hide. There was no railroad and no roads passing through. Everything dead-ended here which meant that nobody came unless they had business.

Last night, everybody had been wondering what his business was. Today, they knew. Or if they all didn't, at least one of them did.

It had been careless of him to leave that roll of posters where they could be found. He should have kept them with him, in his saddlebags. But it was too late now to change anything. Someone knew he was a bounty hunter. That someone was wanted and would try to kill him before he caught up with him.

A mile above town, he found the road and turned into it. From habit, he studied its surface. One set of tracks was fresh, apparently having been made during the night. All the others were blurred, baked by the sun yesterday and made indistinct by wind.

At a walk, Dunbar rode north. A certain wariness had come to him. There were dozens of places along this road where he could be ambushed, he thought. The road descended into the wash and climbed out again every half mile or so. Greasewood was as high as a man's head on horseback. Smaller dry washes occasionally fed into the main one on the valley floor.

Dunbar tried to remember the faces and names that had been on the wanted posters. His memory was excellent and he had studied the posters so many times that he pretty much knew each face and the name that went with it. He knew the bounty on each wanted man and, more important, he knew the crime of which each was accused. In that bundle had been posters on several murderers, men who wouldn't hesitate to kill again if they were threatened or if they thought they were.

The first house he passed was a single room adobe shack with a sod roof out of which high, dry weeds grew. It was no more than a quarter mile from the road and he could see no sign of life.

The sun was well up into the sky by now and it was getting hot. Dunbar pulled his hat lower in front to shield his eyes from its glare, and went on. The second house was built of old railroad ties and was a little bigger than the adobe shack, but not much. It also had a sod roof. A few white chickens scratched industriously in the yard.

The third house was more than a mile beyond. It sat all by itself near the bank of the wash about half a mile from the road. There were chickens around it too, and there was a line stretched between house and outhouse with clothes fluttering from it.

Dunbar felt something churning in his stomach as he turned into the lane and opened the gate. It wasn't nausea, but it was an empty feeling that was unpleasant even if it wasn't unfamiliar. He always got this feeling when he closed with one of the men he was hunting. Maybe it was excitement, tension, or maybe it was fear. He didn't know. He wasn't afraid of Daisy Elbert, but he sure wasn't looking forward to meeting her.

When he was halfway to the house, a dog came out from behind it and began to bark at him. He saw the door open and briefly saw a spot of bright blue in it, a woman's dress, he supposed. It disappeared immediately.

When he rode into the yard, the dog was bristling, barking now almost frantically and backing toward the door. He rode to the door and sat there while the dog circled his nervous horse, his barks even shriller now.

Once more the woman came to the door but this time she stepped outside. Behind her, a boy stood in the doorway, a boy of about nine, wearing ragged woolen pants and a shirt that had plainly been cut down for him.

Dunbar took off his hat. "Good morning, ma'am."

She held a rifle in her hands, its barrel

pointing at the ground at his horse's feet. It was rusty and old and he doubted if it was loaded but even so he didn't intend to make any moves that might startle her.

She was a pretty woman, perhaps thirty-five. Her skin was dark from the sun, and weathered enough to give it little crow's feet at the corners of her eyes. Her mouth was full and unsmiling, but it had a sweetness to it that made him hate to take his eyes from it. When he raised his glance, he saw that her eyes were cold. "What do you want?" she asked.

Her voice was filled with hostility. He said, "I've come a far piece to see you, ma'am. Do you mind if I get down?"

She hesitated a moment. Finally she shrugged. "It's a free country."

He dismounted, from long habit withdrawing his rifle from its scabbard as he did. The gun muzzle raised ever so slightly. Now it was pointing at his knees. He said, "Ma'am, would you mind putting that thing away?"

"Any reason why I should?"

He said, "I don't mean you no harm, ma'am. I come about your man."

"About Frank? He's dead."

"I know that, ma'am."

She lowered the gun but she did not put it down. Nor did she invite him to come into the house. Turning her head she said, "Luke, you get the grease can and climb that windmill. It's squeaking something terrible."

He didn't move. "Me, can't I stay? I . . ."

Her voice turned sharp. "You mind, boy! Now!"

Luke Elbert came out of the house. He looked at Dunbar curiously. He shuffled toward the barn, which was not much bigger than the house and little more than a shelter. Daisy Elbert looked at Dunbar. "What about Frank, mister?"

He said, "My name's Dunbar. Ross Dunbar." He hated to say it but sooner or later it had to be said. "I'm the one that killed him, ma'am."

Her expression didn't change. It remained hostile. If anything her eyes were colder than before.

He turned toward his horse. Her rifle raised warningly. He got his saddlebags from behind the saddle. "He had some money on him. I didn't reckon it would ever get to you if I left it up to the sheriff where he was killed so I brought it here myself."

She studied him, silent for a time. There was a suspicious look to her eyes and something else that didn't make him feel very proud of himself. Finally she said, "And it eases your conscience to come here with Frank's money. Is that it?"

He opened his mouth to deny it, but stopped before he said anything. Looking inward, he supposed that she was right. He probably did want to ease his conscience. He said, "I'm sorry." He knelt to open the saddlebags and get the money out. Something hit the wall of the shack with a sound like the smack of a beaver's tail on the surface of a pond. Dunbar didn't have to be told what it was. He knew before the rifle's sharp, cracking report reached his ears.

And he was moving. From a crouched position, he lunged toward Daisy Elbert. He struck her in the stomach with his shoulder and carried her back into the cabin with the force of his rush. The rifle flew out of her hands and Dunbar sprawled on top of her on the cabin floor. He still had his rifle and the saddlebags.

He caught a glimpse of her face as he pushed himself away from her. It was pale with fright and her eyes were wide with it. As he crawled toward the door, Dunbar said, "That was a shot, ma'am. Fired at me. I'm sorry if I hurt you. Will the boy stay put?"

She was gasping, trying to catch the breath that had been knocked out of her. He didn't look at her, giving her time to regain her composure. Then he repeated urgently, "Will the boy stay put?"

She got to her feet and went toward the door. He got up, caught her arm and pulled her to one side. He said, "Just yell out to him. Don't show yourself."

She called in a voice that was shrill with fear, "Luke?"

The boy answered from up on the windmill. "What, Ma?"

"You stay where you are! They ain't after us!"

The boy didn't answer. Dunbar asked, "Will he stay?"

"He'll stay."

"All right then." He pointed toward the front corner of the room. "Get over there."

She obeyed. After a moment she asked, "What do they want? The money?"

"No ma'am." He picked up a homemade stool and threw it out the door. Instantly a different rifle barked. This time the bullet tore splinters from the doorjamb. Whoever it was with that particular rifle was nervous and trigger-happy and that made him doubly dangerous. Dunbar said, "They're after me."

"Why?"

"Because they're wanted and they think I'm after them."

"You're a lawman then? Is that how you came to kill Frank?"

He shook his head. "No ma'am."

"Then why . . . ?"

He said brutally, "For the money. I hunt men down when there's a reward for them. I'm what they call a bounty man."

She did not reply and he didn't look at her. He didn't have to. He had seen the way people looked at him before when he told them what he was. But for some reason or other, he didn't want to see that look on Daisy Elbert's face.

Chapter 5

For a few minutes Dunbar stood beside the door staring out at the bleak landscape. He knew that the two bullets had come from different guns. The sound of the two reports had been different. He was lucky the first bullet hadn't killed him. If he hadn't knelt to get Frank Elbert's money out of his saddlebags, he'd be lying out there dead right now.

He'd had close calls before, but not many closer than this. He realized that he had begun to sweat just from thinking about it. Wryly he thought that he must be losing his nerve, but even as he thought that he knew it wasn't so. Anybody could break into a sweat realizing that only a sudden, unexpected movement had saved his life.

Daisy Elbert's breathing had become regular again. Dunbar asked, "Did I hurt you?"

Her voice was cold. "I can't say I feel better than I did before."

"Sorry. The second shot might've hit you and I reckon that would've hurt some worse."

"What are *you* going to do? I don't want you here."

"There ain't nothing I can do, ma'am, as long as it's light. There's two of them. They'd cut me down before I'd gone ten feet."

"So you're going to wait here until it gets dark?"

"I guess I'll have to, ma'am."

"I'm worried about my son."

"They won't hurt him, ma'am." Dunbar made his voice sound confident but he was not as confident as he tried to sound. They could threaten to shoot the boy unless he came out. If that happened . . . Hell, he thought irritably, he didn't know what he'd do until the situation stared him in the face. There was no use sitting here making trouble up. There was plenty without making up any more.

Suddenly, from outside, Dunbar heard young Luke's voice. "Ma?"

She headed toward the door. Dunbar stopped her before she could show herself. She screamed, "Luke? You stay there!"

"Can't I come down, Ma? Can't I come in the house?"

"You stay where you are! They . . ." Dunbar clamped a hand over her mouth. "Don't give 'em any ideas, ma'am." He took the hand away and she called, "Just mind me, hear?"

Luke didn't reply. Dunbar wished he'd kept that bunch of wanted posters in his saddlebags. If he had, he could get them out now and show them to Daisy and probably figure out who was shooting at him.

The saddlebags lay in the middle of the floor where he and Daisy Elbert had sprawled earlier. Dunbar put out a foot and hooked them with his toe. He pulled them toward him. The movement, dimly seen, drew another bullet, which struck the floor where the saddlebags had been. The impact raised a little plume of dust from the cracks between the boards.

Dunbar opened the saddlebag that contained the sack of gold. He got it out, straightened up and held it out to her. He said, "I ain't counted it, but there must be five or six hundred dollars."

She made no move to take the sack. "I don't want it," she said.

He said, "It ain't the money that was on your husband's head, if that's what's troublin' you. I got that, an' I figure it was rightly mine."

Still she didn't take the sack, so he tossed it toward her. She caught it out of pure reflex, then frowned at him for tricking her into taking it. He said, "I can't blame you for not likin' me bein' as I killed your man." He felt a sudden compulsion to justify himself, and wondered mildly at it. It was the first time since he'd taken up hunting men that he'd ever felt that need. He said, "I want you to know, ma'am, that I didn't kill him needlessly. I called out to him. I told him who I was and I told him I had a poster on him and was taking him in. He . . ." He stopped, wondering if, to justify himself, he was justified in destroying Frank Elbert in the eyes of his wife. Daisy Elbert said, "He what?"

"I don't reckon it matters now."

She said, "It matters. I want to know the truth for once."

Dunbar shrugged. "All right. He said he

51

was coming out. He was over behind some rocks, along with his played-out horse. He come out, all right, and so did I. He'd throwed down his rifle. He had his hands up in the air. Then real quick he went for a gun he had in his belt underneath his coat. First shot missed. I didn't wait for the second one."

Daisy Elbert said, "How do I know you're telling me the truth?" Her voice was skeptical.

"You don't. But you knowed your husband a heap better than I ever did. You know whether he'd do what I said he done."

"Whether he would and whether he did are two different things."

"Sure. So I reckon you just got to make up your mind whether I lied to you or not."

"Why didn't you have the money sent?"

"Well, ma'am, I've knowed a lot of small town sheriffs in my time. Lots of times they use the money an outlaw's got on him for buryin'. Or maybe they give it to somebody that says he robbed from them. Sometimes it just disappears whilst they're countin' it."

"And you always take an outlaw's money to his next of kin?"

"No ma'am, I don't."

"Then why did you bring it to me?

Because your conscience is troubling you?''

Dunbar thought about that. He nodded. ''Maybe. Maybe away down deep I figured I could've held off a couple of seconds more. Your husband might've dropped that gun when he seen he'd missed.''

She said, ''He might. I guess that's something you got to live with—wondering whether he would or not. Anyhow, I figure there's something wrong with a man that hunts other men for the money rewards put up on them.''

He started to defend himself, then closed his mouth. Outside, a voice yelled, ''Come on out, bounty man! Unless you want Miz Elbert an' her boy gettin' hurt!''

Dunbar glanced at Daisy. Her face was pale now and her eyes were wide. He said, ''They won't . . .''

Suddenly both rifles opened up outside the cabin. Bullets came in through the open door. Some went harmlessly into the floor. Others smashed dishes in the cabinet on the far wall. Still others clanged thunderously against the stove and ricocheted. Dunbar ducked involuntarily. The fusillade continued until the rifles were empty. The same voice yelled, ''You comin' out?''

Dunbar glanced at Daisy again. She was

looking at the wreckage of her dishes with dismay. She caught his glance, held it a minute and shook her head. "Don't go out. I don't like you but I don't want you killed on my account."

"Recognize that voice?"

She said, "It could be Grady Morse. He used to stay here once in a while. Until I told him not to come any more."

Dunbar remembered a poster with the name Grady Morse on it. There had been another man wanted along with him. The charge had been murder and stagecoach robbery. The pair had probably found out from whoever had gone through his bedroll that he was a bounty hunter and they thought he was after them. It was ironic in a way. If they'd just sat tight for another day, he'd have been gone.

Daisy Elbert asked, "Is he wanted?"

"Yes ma'am."

"What for?"

"Murder and stagecoach robbery."

"And his friend? Ed Huett?"

"He's likely wanted too, although I ain't real sure."

She was silent for a moment. When she spoke, finally, her voice was touched with anger. "Did it ever occur to you that the men you hunt may be changed? That they may be living honest lives?"

He said, "People got to pay for what they do."

"Even if they've changed? Even if they're living honest lives?"

He said harshly, "Them two out there ain't changed. Right now they're tryin' to murder me and they wouldn't mind too much if they killed you doing it."

"But . . ."

Still harshly, he asked, "Was your husband changed? Would he ever have changed?"

She didn't answer and he didn't expect her to. But he realized suddenly that for some reason he wanted this woman to like him. He wanted her to believe that what he did for a living was necessary and right. He said, "Six years ago two men rode into the ranch where my brother lived. He had a wife and his son was about the age of your boy out there. He had less'n a hundred dollars, but they killed him and his wife and boy for it. They didn't have to kill. I knowed him and he wouldn't have held out and risked his family's lives for a hundred dollars."

Daisy said, "I'm sorry," but there was no sympathy in her voice.

"I ain't telling it to get your sympathy. The trail was two days old when I found them there. I buried them and went to the county seat for the sheriff. He took a whole day gettin' up a posse and then he wouldn't go no farther than the county line. Said the trail was cold and he'd never catch up with 'em and besides he didn't have no jurisdiction outside his county."

He stared blankly at the wall, remembering. "I took the trail alone. Big rain came up and washed it out. I kept goin', but I never did find it again."

She was silent, not looking at him.

"Well, what I'm gettin' at is why I started doing what I do. I don't know them killers' names and I don't know what they look like, but I figured if the law wouldn't go after killers like they was supposed to do, then maybe it was time somebody else took it on hisself. I went back to that sheriff's office and got all the posters he had and started out. I used the first rewards I earned to put up a bounty on the men that killed my brother and his family. Likely it won't ever be claimed unless one of 'em talks about it when he's drunk. But I figure by catching the other men I've caught maybe I've kept that kind of thing from happenin' to other folks."

Once more the voice outside the cabin yelled, "You comin' out, bounty man?"

He didn't reply. He turned to catch her terrified gaze. "What if they shoot at Luke up there on the windmill?"

"They won't." But he wasn't sure. The two rifles opened up again and once more bullets came tearing in through the open door, to rip splinters from the floor, to clang against the stove, to shatter more dishes in the cabinet. It was wanton destruction, pure viciousness. Dunbar wanted to go to the door and at least return their fire. He didn't because he knew it would only make things worse.

He began to pray silently that they wouldn't get the idea of threatening Luke in an effort to make him show himself. If they did he'd have to go outside. Even if it resulted in his death, he'd have to go outside.

Chapter 6

Grady Morse was a short and thickset man, almost totally bald. His face wore a five-day growth of whiskers beginning to show a little gray. Their shack on the unnamed wash north of the town of Dry Creek was only a place to hide as far as he was concerned. He liked towns, and company, and women. He didn't know how that bounty hunter found them here but he meant to see that the son-of-a-bitch didn't leave the Elbert cabin alive.

Ed Huett was sprawled behind a clump of greasewood a hundred and fifty yards away. At intervals, they both opened up on the cabin, putting bullets in through the door in the hope that a ricochet would catch their man.

The sun sank steadily in the western sky. Morse knelt at the side of the dry wash, his rifle poking up over its edge. In the airless bottom of the wash he guessed it must be well over a hundred degrees. He sweated until his clothes were soaked and as his discomfort increased his disposition grew worse.

He could see young Luke Elbert on the windmill platform. Luke was sitting down, his back to one of the timbers, partially at least, in the shade. He could tell there was a breeze up there because the blades of the windmill turned lazily. A trickle of water pumped by its action dribbled into the tank at its foot.

Every time Morse thought of how close he'd come to killing the bounty hunter with his first shot, he got furious. The bullet had been well aimed. All that had saved the bounty man was the fact that, just as he had fired, Dunbar had stooped to get something out of his saddlebags.

Now all they could do was wait. The bounty hunter would come out when it was dark enough. It was up to them to see that he didn't get away when he did.

Huett called, "Grady?"

"What?"

"How we gonna get the son-of-a-bitch out of there?"

"We ain't. We got to wait for dark."

"He'll get away."

"Not if we work in close after the sun goes down. He ain't showed hisself so far an' he ain't likely to."

"What if he makes it to his horse before we get to him?"

"He won't." But Morse began thinking about that. If the bounty hunter had found them here, he had to be pretty smart. Maybe smart enough to get them one by one. The reward poster on them said DEAD OR ALIVE. That gave the bounty man a lot of leeway he otherwise might not have had.

He stared at the bounty hunter's horse, standing hipshot in the yard, reins trailing. The horse seemed half asleep. His head was down and he hadn't moved, except to swish his tail at flies, for a long, long time.

Morse admitted there was a chance the hunter might reach his horse before they could shoot him down. And if he did, there was a good chance he'd get away. Well, by God, he could prevent that easily enough.

He raised his rifle slightly. He rested it on

the tip of the wash to steady it and took careful aim. He aimed at the horse's neck just above the shoulder and carefully squeezed off the shot.

He could hear the bullet hit. It had a curious, slapping sound that was unmistakable. The horse stood there for a moment as if nothing had happened. Then his head sank even lower. He went to his knees.

He stayed in that position for a moment, then collapsed heavily onto his side. He kicked spasmodically several times and then lay still.

Morse raised his point of aim to the doorway, knowing the deliberate killing of his horse might anger the bounty hunter enough to make him reckless. Sure enough it did. The man appeared at the edge of the doorway, rifle poked out in front of him.

Grady took careful aim once more. He fired, squeezing the trigger off slowly. He saw the bounty hunter flinch and he knew he had hit the man.

But the bounty hunter had seen the puff of smoke from his gun. Almost instantly a bullet plowed a furrow in the ground directly in front of Morse, filling his eyes and nose and mouth with dirt. He released his rifle and slid down into the bottom of the wash, cursing and knuckling his eyes.

He heard Huett's gun, and, immediately afterward, the bounty man's gun again. Huett yelled with pain, and then began to swear.

With his eyes partially cleared, Morse clawed up the side of the wash and retrieved his gun. He was mad now. Sticking his head up above the wash, he emptied his rifle into the doorway of the cabin. The bounty hunter ducked back and did not appear again.

Morse laid the rifle down and slid to the bottom of the wash a second time. His eyes were streaming and tears ran along his dirty cheeks. He began to cough, clearing nose and throat of the dirt the bullet had kicked up.

He pulled a dirty bandanna out of his pocket and tried to clear his eyes. At least that damned bounty hunter wasn't going anywhere. When it got dark, they'd go down and finish him off, once and for all.

Dunbar heard the shot that struck his horse. He also heard, just before he heard the report, the unmistakable sound a bullet makes striking solid flesh. He peered out, saw his horse's head sink lower and saw him go to his knees. He knew that in Morse's shoes he'd have done the same thing, unhesitatingly, yet having it done to him made him furious. He poked his rifle around the doorjamb and waited for the smoke puff from the muzzle of one of the guns out there.

He saw the puff from Morse's gun, and at almost the same instant felt the bullet burn the muscles of his upper arm. He fired instantly and saw the dust kicked up by the bullet. Smoke puffed from the other rifle, this bullet going past him harmlessly. He fired again and was rewarded by the second man's high yell. But the man didn't raise up, and he had nothing further at which to shoot.

He pulled back. Daisy Elbert said, "You're hit."

"Ain't much."

"Let me look at it.' She came toward him and he said gruffly, "Forget it."

She asked irritably, "Do you think I want you bleeding all over my floor?"

He said, "All right. Tie it up so it won't bleed all over everything." He took off his shirt and shrugged out of the upper half of his underwear to expose the wound.

It was a ragged gash, half an inch wide and a couple of inches long. There were bits of shredded cloth in it, and it looked like it had been made by a saw instead of by a bullet. It was bleeding copiously. Daisy Elbert's face whitened but she didn't flinch. She said, "Sit down and be still. I'll get some whiskey and some bandages."

Daisy came back, a piece of clean white cloth in one hand, a brown bottle of whiskey in the other one. She removed the cork from the bottle, but before she could wash the wound with it, Dunbar took it from her and put it to his mouth. He took a drink and handed it back. She tore off a piece of the cloth, soaked it with whiskey and began to sponge off the wound.

Dunbar gritted his teeth and gripped the sides of the stool with both hands. He swayed and she steadied him. "Are you going to be all right?"

"Yes ma'am. I'm dizzy is all. Go ahead."

She crossed the room and threw the bloody cloth into the stove, staying close against the rear wall so that her movement wouldn't catch the notice of the men outside. She returned, tore a pad from the cloth and put it on the wound. Blood soaked it almost immediately. She tore strips of cloth and when she judged she had enough, began to wrap them around Dunbar's upper arm, tight enough to eventually stop the bleeding but not tight enough to impair circulation. By the time she had finished, Dunbar was lightheaded and weak. She handed him the bottle and he took another drink.

He shrugged into his blood-soaked underwear, grimacing with the pain when he moved the wounded arm. He put on his shirt and got to his feet. For a moment the room whirled. Then it steadied.

Daisy Elbert moved toward the back of the room to put away the whiskey and bandage material. Dunbar moved close to the doorway and cautiously peered outside.

The sun was setting. It cast long shadows from windmill, house, and barn. He knew they'd expect him to leave as soon as it was dark. They'd have moved in close and the instant he showed himself they'd riddle him.

His horse suddenly drew his glance. The animal wasn't dead. He could see the rise and fall of the horse's side and the animal suddenly began to kick feebly with one hind foot.

Dunbar stepped back away from the door. He spoke to Daisy over a shoulder. "The horse ain't dead. I'm going to shoot him and the shot will probably draw some return fire from them. Get over here beside me just in case."

She obeyed. Dunbar aimed carefully at his horse's head behind the ears. He fired. The horse's head jerked, but the kicking ceased.

The shot drew the expected response. Both rifles outside opened up and once more bullets came tearing in through the cabin's open door.

The sun, by now, was down. Overhead, the few puffy clouds turned a brilliant orange, then gold, then slowly began to fade. Dunbar said, "Call out to your boy. Tell him to stay where he is until you tell him to come down."

She moved up beside him. Her head, he noticed, came just to the point of his shoulder. She smelled fresh and clean. She called, "Luke!"

"What?"

"You stay up there until I tell you to come down."

He did not reply.

She called, "Luke?"

"All right," he called grudgingly.

She said, "He'll stay."

Outside the sky was gray. Dunbar knew his only chance was to move before the two men expected it. They'd count on him to wait until it was completely dark. But there was a period just before that when most of the light would have faded from the sky, when objects would be visible but when it would be too dark to clearly see the sights of a gun. That period was when he would have to go.

Daisy said grudgingly, "Be careful."

He glanced at her, surprised. Her face was just a blur now. He said, "I will."

She said reluctantly and with weary disillusionment, "Frank never would have dropped his gun. He'd have killed you if you had not killed him."

He didn't answer her because there didn't seem to be anything appropriate for him to say. She had told him, in those few words, that she bore no grudge. She had admitted that her husband was treacherous but it was time now for him to go. Or almost time. He swiftly reloaded his rifle, jacked a cartridge into the chamber and stepped toward the door. He turned his head to look at her, wishing there was enough light to tell what expression was on her face.

He lunged toward the doorway. He went through it on a dead run, bent halfway over, and immediately skidded into a right-angle turn.

There was an instant when nothing happened, when the silence was eerie and unnatural. Then, Dunbar heard a shout. A gun flashed. A bullet struck the ground behind him, ricocheted and whined away. A second gun began firing.

But Dunbar was in the clear, running, still bent over to present as small a target as possible. He reached the greasewood at the edge of the clearing unhit. Behind him he could hear Morse's shouts, giving directions to Huett for heading him off.

He didn't make the mistake of under-estimating them. They were dangerous and they were scared. If he didn't get them first, they would get him. He had escaped the cabin, but he was afoot out here half a dozen miles from town. His chances of getting another horse were slim. Morse and Huett would be guarding theirs.

He ran swiftly, silently and tirelessly and at last, behind him, he heard the galloping pound of hoofs.

The trouble was, there was still a little light. It wasn't dark enough to hide.

Chapter 7

As soon as he heard the hoofbeats, he stopped. Trying to hide wasn't going to solve his problem. Huett and Morse weren't going to let him leave the country alive and hiding, even if he did it successfully, would only postpone the inevitable.

He became a shadow, like an Indian stalking game. He moved away at right angles to the course he had been traveling. His revolver was in its holster, his rifle in his hand. He knew there was a cartridge in the chamber and the hammer was on full cock. Closer came the hoofbeats, and he could track the pair pursuing him by the sound. When the noise told him they were within sight of him, he stopped, standing motionless beside a tall clump of greasewood.

They were galloping recklessly, about ten yards apart. He didn't move. The light was too poor to see the sights of his gun and if he gambled on hitting one of them and missed, they'd both turn on him.

So he held his fire, waited, and let them go on past. The sound of their horses' hoofs faded and silence fell over the heavy brush. It still was hot, but a slight breeze was beginning to stir in the west.

Dunbar's wounded arm ached. He moved it back and forth, exercising it to keep it from going stiff. Huett and Morse would return when they realized he was no longer ahead of them. If he was lucky, they'd come one at a time and if they did, he'd maybe risk a shot, poor light and all.

It was quiet for what must have been ten minutes or more. Then, unexpectedly, he heard a branch crack, and a moment later heard the jingle of metal against metal.

It was darker now. Only the slightest line of gray remained in the west. Stars had come out, but they gave off little light. His eyes caught a blur of black against the sky, a temporary blotting out of the stars.

It was closer than he had expected, close

enough to fire, yet he knew there was no way of being sure of hitting what he pointed at and it was much too dark to aim.

Six years of hunting the most dangerous game there was helped him now. Dropping the rifle, he leaped, like a predator leaping upon its catch. He collided with the horse, which shied and dug hoofs into the dirt to run. But Dunbar had his man by an arm and his dead weight dragged the rider from the saddle. Both of them hit the ground in a clump of thorny greasewood with a crash that must have been audible for a hundred yards. Dunbar wasted no time struggling with the man. That would have put him at the mercy of the other one. Instead, he tore loose, fought his way out of the greasewood clump, and dived for his rifle, lying where he had dropped it ten feet away.

His hand closed on it as the other man clawed his way out of the thorny greasewood clump. The outlaw's handgun roared, echoing Dunbar's rifle. He heard the man howl as the bullet struck him, then heard his progress as he fled in frantic fear.

Dunbar began thinking of the other one, the hoofbeats of whose horse were now a growing thunder in the ground.

From his crouch Dunbar raised up enough

to bring his rifle into play. Once more he saw the blur of darkness against the stars. Sound and sight told him the horse was no more than ten yards away, yet he waited, waited until the animal was almost on top of him.

He fired, then, and saw the lance-like tongue of bluish flame that shot from the muzzle of his gun. He didn't hear the bullet hit because the horse and rider were too close and because the report drowned out that distinctive sound. But he knew the bullet hit. The horse stumbled, and came somersaulting toward him, a giant, overwhelming weight, and he threw himself to one side, rifle still clutched in one hand, shoulder burning ferociously when a flying hoof struck it a glancing blow.

Down went the horse, skidding through the heavy brush. The rider sailed clear over his head, landing in another clump of brush twenty feet away.

Dunbar fought to his feet. The horse still kicked but he was wounded mortally. A wheezing sound came from his throat that drowned out all other sound.

Dunbar waited there, listening, trying to hear the sounds made by the horse's rider, failing because of the racket made by the horse. He didn't dare finish off the animal.

That would give his position away and draw fire from the other man.

Breathing shallowly and moving a careful step at a time, Dunbar eased away from the wounded horse. With each step he took, the wheezing sound diminished. But he could still hear no other sound.

Fifty yards from the horse, he stopped. His foot had stirred a rock and now he stooped and picked it up. It was half the size of his fist. He drew back his arm and threw it toward the place where the horse's rider had landed earlier.

Nothing happened. He heard no sound. The sudden noise drew no gunfire.

Dunbar released a long, slow sigh of relief. But he did not yet relax his vigilance, knowing this game well. His prey might have withheld his fire deliberately to lull Dunbar into making his position known.

He hunkered down, laying his rifle carefully on the ground immediately at his side. He let himself go loose, but listened intently all the time.

The horse's wheezes were growing faint and he was not kicking any more. Dunbar wished he could have killed the horse and put it out of its misery but that had been impossible.

Ten minutes he waited, as patiently as an animal. Ten more minutes passed. The horse had stopped wheezing now and was completely still. At last, after thirty minutes of utter silence, he picked up his rifle and got stiffly to his feet. Silent, still moving like an Indian, he headed back toward Daisy Elbert's cabin. He had to have a horse to get back to town. Maybe she'd lend him one.

The cabin was dark as he approached. He did not call out, knowing one or both of the outlaws might be inside, holding Daisy Elbert and Luke prisoner, waiting for him to return. Instead, he picked up a small stone and tossed it at the cabin. It struck the window and almost immediately Daisy Elbert's voice called, "Who's there? Who is it?"

He knew she would not have used those words had Morse and Huett been inside. He called, "It's Ross Dunbar, ma'am. I reckon it's safe to light the lamp."

A match flared inside the cabin, and a moment later lamplight lit the window and open door. Dunbar approached, not entirely relaxed yet, but reasonably sure Morse and Huett had gone. They were down to a single horse and one of them was wounded. They wouldn't give up, but they'd probably had enough for now.

He stepped in through the door. Daisy's face was pale and her eyes were scared.

He said, "I hit one of them, but I doubt if he's hurt very bad. I killed the other one's horse. I figure they've gone home."

She was looking at Luke, frowning because Luke was staring with open admiration. Dunbar said, "I'm sorry I brought all this trouble to you. I'll pay for the damage they did to your dishes and things."

She turned her back and went to the stove. Luke asked, "Why are they tryin' to kill you, mister?"

Dunbar hesitated, afraid that answering might lead him into having to tell the boy why he was here. He looked down into Luke's young face. He couldn't recall ever having had anyone look at him quite the way Luke was looking at him now. Shaken by such unabashed admiration, he said, "They're outlaws, son. They thought I was after them."

"Was you?"

"No. I wasn't. But now I am."

"You a lawman, mister?"

"Kind of, I guess."

Daisy must have noticed the direction the

conversation was going because she said impatiently, "Luke, let Mr. Dunbar alone."

"I ain't botherin' him, Ma. Am I, Mister Dunbar?"

"Better mind your ma, son."

Before Luke could protest, Mrs. Elbert said, "I suppose you'd might as well stay to supper, now that you're here."

He was, for an instant, too startled to reply. He mumbled, "I just thought maybe I could borrow a horse to get back to town. I'll return him in the morning and I'll drag that dead horse away when I do."

"You have to eat, and by the time you reach town everything will be closed."

His glance met hers and she quickly looked away. He said, "Thank you, ma'am. I guess I will stay then."

She said, "Luke, go out and wash."

"Yes, ma'am."

Dunbar started to follow Luke but Daisy Elbert said, "Wait. Wait until he's through."

Dunbar waited beside the door. Daisy said, "I . . . wanted to tell you something. In the last six years, my husband was here for a total of five whole days. He didn't even know his son and what's worse he didn't care. I could have forgiven him for neglecting me, but I will never forgive him for neglecting Luke. You saw the way Luke looked at you. He's so starved for the company of a man that I could cry seeing the way he looks at any that bothers to notice him. It was because of him that I asked you to stay."

Dunbar didn't know what to say so he contented himself with murmuring, "Yes, ma'am."

"I don't think much of what you do but I guess I don't hate you for killing Frank. I just wish you hadn't come. I don't want anything of Frank's. We got along without any help from him while he was alive and I figured we could get along without help from him after he was dead."

She stopped speaking as Luke came through the door. His hair was damp but it wasn't combed. Dunbar mussed it briefly as he went out. He crossed the yard to the pipe dribbling into the tank at the windmill's base, and washed his face and hands. He returned to the house, after having dried himself with a flour sack hanging from a nail.

Daisy said, "Sit down, Mr. Dunbar. Would you like a drink?"

"Yes, ma'am."

She brought out the brown bottle of whiskey and set it, and a glass, in front of him. Dunbar poured a drink and sipped it. Across the table, Luke was watching him. He asked, "Don't it taste awful?"

Dunbar grinned. "Awful."

"Then how come you ain't makin' a face?"

Dunbar made a face and Luke grinned at him. After a moment he asked, "You got a horse in the corral I can borrow until tomorrow?"

"He ain't in the corral, but I can get him."

"Mind?"

"No, sir."

Daisy said, "Supper ain't ready yet. Go get him now and milk the cow."

"Aw, Ma, I'll have to wash again."

"Won't hurt you. Get along now."

"Yes, ma'am." Luke took the milk pail and went out.

Dunbar said, "He's a good boy."

"No thanks to his pa."

"He know about his pa?"

"Some. Not all."

For a while they sat in silence that, Dunbar discovered, was companionable. And once more the ache that was becoming all too familiar came to him. Frank Elbert had been a fool. He'd had this and he'd stayed away from it and he'd ended up getting himself killed. By a man, Dunbar thought wryly, who would have given anything to have what he didn't want.

Daisy asked, "What will you do when you've caught them?"

"Take them back. Collect the reward."

"And then?"

"I don't know. But I'm through hunting men. Maybe I'll buy myself a ranch. I've got enough to buy one and stock it good."

To himself he was thinking that before he bought a ranch he might just come back here even if it didn't do any good.

He made himself think of Huett and Morse instead of Daisy and her son. He could get himself killed mooning over a woman he couldn't have. He ought to have his thoughts on his business.

Chapter 8

While Daisy Elbert fixed supper, consisting of fried deer meat and fried potatoes, Dunbar sat indolently at the table. His shoulder burned ferociously but he tried not to think of it. It was a flesh wound. It might stiffen his arm and make him uncomfortable, but unless it festered it wasn't serious.

He watched her, enjoying, despite her obvious dislike of him, the sight of a woman doing a woman's work. She was shapely and clean and he remembered the way she had smelled. Once more he thought that Frank Elbert had been a fool. He briefly indulged in the fantasy that Daisy might someday be his, that this could be what he did every night instead of bedding down alone on the prairie or in the mountains, to continue some manhunt the day following.

He heard the tinkle of the cow's bell, and after a while Luke came in, lugging a milk pail that was about half full. He put it down and went out to wash his hands again. Daisy strained the milk through a clean flour sack, then set it outside to cool.

Luke came back in. He looked at Dunbar, but when Dunbar caught his glance, he looked away again. The boy thought he was really something now, Dunbar thought. But what about when he found out Dunbar had killed his pa? The boy would hate him bitterly. He'd never be reconciled to having the killer of his father take that father's place, even if his mother would.

Dunbar realized he had been foolish to even think it was possible. Daisy was a beautiful woman and she could have any man she wanted. She didn't have to take a footloose bounty hunter, turned cynical and hard by the work he did.

She brought a platter of venison and another of fried potatoes. Dunbar finished his drink. She sat down across from him and looked at Luke. Luke bowed his head. He said, "Lord, we thank you for this here food. Amen.''

Daisy said, ''It's not much. But it's better than nothing I guess.''

Dunbar said, ''It's fine. It smells delicious.''

''We live on deer meat. We can't afford to kill what little beef we have.''

''How many *do* you have?''

Luke answered for her. ''We got nineteen cows. But someday we're goin' to have a thousand of 'em an' maybe more. Then we're goin' to build a big new house. We're goin' to have hired hands, an' Ma's goin' to have someone to help her out.''

Daisy smiled at Luke. Dunbar thought it was a pity Luke's father hadn't shared some of his ambition and concern. He said, ''A thousand cows is a lot of work.''

Luke swallowed the meat he had in his mouth. ''I ain't afraid of work. I take care of them nineteen cows an' their calves. When I'm bigger I can do more.''

Daisy nodded. ''He does do a man's work. I couldn't get along without him.''

Luke looked at Dunbar. ''What about you, Mister Dunbar? You goin' to catch them two that was shootin' at you?''

''If I can.''

''Maybe that's what I'll do when I grow

up. Maybe I'll chase down killers like what you do. You reckon I could?"

Dunbar said, "You can do anything you want. But I'd say having a thousand cows would be better than runnin' outlaws down."

"Not as much fun though. I bet you've killed lots of men."

Dunbar took a bite of meat and chewed without answering. He didn't like the way the conversation was heading.

Luke asked, "How many men you killed, Mr. Dunbar?"

Dunbar said shortly, "I don't keep count." His mind was on this boy's father and once more he could almost see the man, could remember the surprised look that had been on Frank Elbert's face as he died.

Daisy said sharply, "Don't you be pesterin' Mr. Dunbar now. You eat an' let him be."

Dunbar finished his food. He was very uneasy and very uncomfortable. He waited until Daisy Elbert had finished eating and then stood up. "I got to get back to town. I'll come out in the morning and drag that horse away. You got a team?"

She nodded. "Luke will bring them in first thing in the morning."

Luke said, "I can drag that old horse off."

Dunbar thought he probably could. He was sturdy and competent and he was going to grow up to be one hell of a man. But Dunbar wanted to come back. He said, "I'll come and help."

"Yes, sir," said the boy. Dunbar picked up his hat. Daisy Elbert came to the door with him. Dunbar went out into the yard and pulled the saddle off his horse. He got the bridle and put both bridle and saddle on the horse Luke had caught for him. He got his rifle from beside the door where he had leaned it as he went in. He shoved it into the saddle boot.

He mounted and touched the brim of his hat. "Ma'am, I'm obliged—for the supper and everything. And I'm sorry I brought all this trouble down on you. I figure to pay for them dishes that got broke. And whatever else."

He rode away, turning once when he was hidden by darkness and looking back. Daisy stood in the doorway, slim and pretty, with Luke beside her. The sight of the two of them put the old ache in Dunbar and he looked away angrily. He was a damn fool. He didn't even know the woman. What he did know was that her son would never accept him once the boy knew he was the one who had killed his pa. Luke likely wouldn't know what kind of man his father had been. His mother wouldn't have told him that. And Dunbar couldn't tell him. He couldn't even in an attempt to justify himself.

Briefly he thought that tomorrow he'd get the liveryman to ride up and drag the dead horse off. He'd send along a couple of double eagles to pay for the damages. He'd get out of town.

Then his shoulder gave him a twinge of pain and he remembered Huett and Morse. He couldn't leave. Not until he had taken care of them. To leave now would be to put Daisy Elbert in jeopardy. She knew that Morse and Huett had reward posters out on them. They'd be afraid she'd tell the sheriff unless they made sure she didn't have the chance. Which meant Luke was in equal danger from the pair.

He reached town around ten o'clock. The saloon was open, its doors still tied back to let in the cooler evening air. A piano tinkled inside the saloon.

Dunbar rode straight to the livery barn. He swung down stiffly, wincing with the pain his shoulder gave him as he twisted it. The liveryman looked at it, seeing the blood that had soaked through his shirt, and the bloody bandage showing through the bullet hole. He said, "What happened to you? That looks like a bullet hole."

Dunbar said, "Folks around here don't seem too hospitable."

"Know who done it?"

"I know."

"Better send for the sheriff."

"I can handle it." Dunbar took his saddlebags. He said, "Feed this horse and rub him down. I'll want to buy another horse from you tomorrow so get two or three good ones in."

"Yes, *sir.*" The liveryman was grinning now. "You couldn't of come to a better place."

Dunbar said, "We'll find that out tomorrow." Carrying his saddlebags, he went toward the door. The liveryman called after him, "You seen Mitch Harrow anyplace?"

Dunbar turned, "Who's Mitch Harrow?"

"Fella lives around here." The liveryman was flustered and obviously now wanted to drop the subject. He said, "Never mind. I just thought you mighta seen him on the road."

Dunbar said, "I don't even know him. Should I?"

The liveryman's hands were shaking now. Dunbar stopped close to him. "Is Mitch Harrow the one who went through my blanket roll?"

"I don't know what you're talkin' about."

Dunbar said, "It was either him or you."

"It was him. I didn't touch your saddle. I swear it!"

"All right. So it was him. What did he want?"

"He wanted to know who you was. That's all."

"And he took a roll of bounty posters, didn't he? Do you let just anybody steal from your customers' saddles?"

"He didn't take nothing. I swear it. I was right here all the time. He looked at that roll of posters an' then he put them back. Honest to God, he put them back!"

Dunbar went into the street and walked toward the hotel. He was worried about Daisy and her son but he knew he couldn't just go spend the night out there. Besides, Huett and Morse would probably try to kill him first and then work it out so they could claim he had killed Daisy and her son, that they'd surprised him doing it and had killed him when he tried to escape.

He went into the hotel lobby. The kid behind the desk wouldn't look at him. Dunbar got his key and went up the stairs.

After Mitch Harrow had left Quirino Madrid sat up most of the night in his darkened shack, trying to decide what he should do. For two years now he had hidden himself here, cut off from family and from friends, afraid to form any new relationships because of the cloud hanging over him.

He realized now that he had been miserable every minute of the time. He was not normally a solitary man and the thought of living out the rest of his life alone suddenly seemed intolerable. Better to be dead than to live like this.

It was almost three in the morning when he finally made up his mind. He would hide himself no more. If the bounty hunter came looking for him, he would surrender himself. Maybe by now the vengefulness of Julio Chavez's father had cooled. Maybe he would admit that the fight in which his son had died had been a fair one and not murder as he first had claimed. Certainly Madrid had no intention of killing again to keep his freedom. One killing, as he had told

Harrow, was enough.

He went to bed and slept, more soundly than he had in months. He did not awaken until the sun was well up into the sky.

The sounds that awakened him were those of two horses riding into the yard. Even after the decision he had made last night, he still was wary as only a hunted man can be and awakened easily at the slightest sound.

He got up, reached for his rifle, then changed his mind. Still in his underwear, he went to the door.

Morse and Huett were standing there. Morse said, "I reckon you know why we're here."

Madrid nodded. He stood aside to let them come in. Morse said, "Harrow brought the posters up last night. Did he stop here?"

Madrid nodded.

Morse said, "We ain't going to just stand by and let that bounty hunter take us back. We're goin' to get him first. You're wanted same as we are. Saddle a horse and come along."

Madrid shook his head.

"Why not? You want to get caught?"

"No. But I will not kill again to keep from getting caught."

Morse scowled and looked at Huett.

Madrid suddenly felt uneasy, as if he could sense something that was in the two men's minds. He asked, "Where is Harrow? Why is he not with you?"

"Hell, that gutless son-of-a-bitch skipped the country last night. He's probably fifty miles away by now."

Madrid didn't know why he suspected it but he did. Harrow wasn't fifty miles away. Harrow was no longer alive.

As he had stepped aside from the doorway to let Morse and Huett in, he had backed against his rifle leaning against the wall. Now, knowing they meant to kill him too, he put a hand behind him and grabbed its barrel. Morse had stepped aside so that Huett would not be directly behind him. Madrid knew it was time. He brought the rifle up and leveled it, jacking in a cartridge as he did. Morse looked startled. "Whatda you doin' that for?"

Madrid said, "Out. And don't come back. You killed Harrow last night, didn't you? Just like you were planning to kill me just now."

"Hell, I don't know what you're talkin' about. Why would we want to kill either you or Harrow? All we want is to be rid of that damned bounty hunter."

But he shuffled out the door, followed by Huett. Madrid held the rifle pointing loosely at them until they had mounted and ridden out of the yard. He watched until they had disappeared.

He knew that now he was faced with a worse dilemma than he had been last night. Morse and Huett, if they did get rid of the bounty hunter, would keep trying until they had succeeded in killing him too because, like Harrow, he knew they were wanted and for what. They'd figure that if he was caught he might give that information away and tell where they were.

Furthermore, if he did nothing, he would have to share the guilt for the bounty hunter's death.

He began to pace impatiently back and forth. He had decided last night that he wouldn't kill again to remain free. But neither did he want to voluntarily surrender himself when he knew that doing so might be the equivalent of committing suicide.

It was a thing he would have to think about, he decided, not a thing to be decided hastily. Frowning, he dressed, ate some bread and drank some wine and saddled up his horse. He rode out, to find and bunch the sheep and drive them down to drink.

Chapter 9

Dunbar sat at the window for a long time, letting the cool evening breeze blow across him. He was sweaty from the heat, and the breeze felt pleasant. He didn't want to go to bed because he knew how hot it would be over in that corner of the room.

He wanted a beer but he didn't want to go downstairs after it. Finally, turned drowsy, he got up. He placed the chair against the door so that it would crash to the floor if the door was opened the slightest bit. He took off his boots and shirt and pants and laid down on top of the bed in his underwear. He placed his revolver close to his hand and closed his eyes. He didn't think Morse and

Huett would try killing him right here in the hotel but he didn't intend to take any chances he didn't have to take.

He awoke with a start at dawn. The chair was still in place before the door. He sat up on the edge of the bed and stared at the gray square of light that marked the window.

The room had cooled considerably during the night. He got up, stretched gingerly, favoring his wounded arm and went to the window. The air was cool and had a clean, fresh smell.

He thought of Daisy Elbert, and knew it was absolutely essential to Daisy's survival that he find the men who had ambushed him there yesterday. He couldn't leave here now even if he wanted to.

He crossed the room, poured water in the basin and washed. He lathered his face and shaved. He put on his shirt, ran his broken piece of comb through his hair and then put on his shirt.

His shoulder was stiff and sore. Movement had started it bleeding again and now the fresh blood was visible on the bandage. He picked up his saddlebags and went downstairs.

There were four other men in the hotel dining room. He sat down after hanging the saddlebags over the back of his chair.

They stared at the saddlebags and they stared at the blood-soaked shoulder of his shirt. But when he caught their glances they looked away.

A young Mexican girl brought him coffee and took his order. After a while she came back with a plate piled high with scrambled eggs, fried potatoes, and smoked ham. He ate hungrily, left a quarter on the table and got up. He picked up his saddlebags and went out through the lobby into the street.

He walked to the livery barn. Fleming, the liveryman, was already there. The sun was just poking above the horizon. Dunbar asked, "Get any horses in?"

"Sure did. Four of 'em. Good ones too. Come on back and take a look."

Dunbar followed him back through the stable to the rear. There were four horses in the corral. None of the four was what he'd consider a fine animal, but one, a hammer-headed gray looked strong and tough. Dunbar took down a rope from a nail on the corral fence, went inside and when the gray pounded past on his second circle of the corral, dropped the loop over his head. The horse stopped. Dunbar walked to him and looked at his teeth. The horse was four or five, he guessed, depending on how much he'd been on rough forage. He lifted the horse's hoofs, one by one, and examined them. He asked, "How much?"

"Hundred and a half."

"I'll give you seventy-five."

"Man, I can't sell him for that. He cost me ninety."

"Seventy-five."

"Give me a hundred."

"Seventy-five."

"All right! All right! You sure drive a hard bargain, friend."

Dunbar led the horse out through the corral gate and into the stable. He bridled him and put his saddle on. He paid the stable fee, gave the liveryman seventy-five dollars for the horse and another dollar for a halter and then, leading Daisy Elbert's horse, he rode out into the street.

He maintained a trot all the way to the Elbert place, arriving when the sun was well up into the sky. Already it was hot, and with the increasing heat his shoulder seemed to pain him more.

Luke came running out to meet him, and when he dismounted said, "I'll put your horse in the barn so's he won't get shot."

Dunbar nodded. The boy led his horse

away and put him in the barn. Dunbar led the horse he had borrowed last night to the corral and turned him in. There was a light team in the corral.

He saw Daisy watching him from the kitchen door. He walked that way and touched the brim of his hat. "Morning, ma'am."

"Good morning, Mr. Dunbar." There seemed to be the slightest change in her manner toward him. She wasn't warm but at least she was no longer so cold.

He said, "Nothing happened last night, did it?"

"No. Have you had breakfast?"

"Yes, ma'am. At the hotel. I'll help Luke hitch up the team and we'll drag that horse away."

He went to the corral, where Luke was already putting halters on the team. Each led one of them to the barn. Dunbar wondered how Luke ever got harness on the horses because he was so short. Maybe his mother helped, he thought. He put the collars on and tossed the harness up. Luke did his share, adjusting it, buckling, straightening out the tugs. He seemed eager for approval and the way he looked at him made Dunbar's throat suddenly feel tight. He let Luke drive the team to where his dead horse lay. He secured a chain around both the dead horse's hind feet. He hooked it to the doubletree. He said, "All right. Drive 'em away."

Luke looked small, too small for the job, but he held the reins and walked beside the dragging horse, staying far enough away so that he wouldn't be caught if the horse rolled suddenly. He headed straight up into the greasewood and sagebrush. When the going got rough, Dunbar took over for him. Between them they dragged the horse nearly a mile from the house before Dunbar judged it was far enough so that the smell wouldn't blow back to the house as the horse decayed.

He boosted Luke up onto one of the horse's backs for the trip back. He walked behind himself letting his eyes scan all the surrounding country from this height. He saw nothing that might betray the presence of Huett and Morse.

When he got to the house, he helped Luke unharness and hang the harness up. Then he walked to the door. Daisy Elbert was standing there, watching him.

Daisy said, "Thank you, Mr. Dunbar."

He said, "I'm going to track those two for a while and see where they went."

"Would you like some coffee before you go?"

He wanted to stay and talk to her, he realized. He nodded. She stepped away from the door and he went in, followed by Luke. He sat down at the table and she brought him some coffee. The destruction caused yesterday by bullets coming in through the open door had all been cleaned up. Dunbar asked, "How many of your dishes did they smash, Mrs. Elbert?"

"Not very many. It wasn't as bad as it sounded at the time."

He fished in his pocket but she said firmly, "I won't accept it, Mr. Dunbar, so don't offer it."

She was flushed and embarrassed and he didn't want to embarrass her further. He sipped the coffee. She got herself a cup and sat down across from him. "Are you going to follow until you catch up with them?"

He shrugged, wincing as he did. "I don't know."

"Can't you just let it go? Nobody was hurt seriously and all you lost was a horse."

He said, "Ma'am, they must know you recognized their voices. They know you know that they're wanted men. Even if I left, you'd still know more about them than they want known."

The color drained out of her face as she realized the implications of what he had said. She glanced quickly at Luke. So did Dunbar, but the boy hadn't been listening closely and apparently didn't understand what Dunbar had been getting at.

She raised her coffee cup with a hand that shook. Dunbar said, "Right now all they're interested in is me. As long as I'm around, there ain't nothing to worry about. If they was to get me, though, I'd suggest you head for the county seat and stay until they're caught."

He had thoroughly frightened her and regretted it, but he knew she'd be safer if she was fully aware of the danger she was in. He finished his coffee and got up. "Thank you, ma'am."

She nodded, preoccupied with her suddenly aroused fears. He went out and mounted his horse. He rode toward the place he had shot one of the pair last night, aware of both Luke and Daisy standing in the yard looking after him.

More now depended on his catching the two wanted men than money, more even than his own safety. Daisy's life and Luke's depended on his success. If he was killed, they would be too.

The realization brought a new sense of caution to him and the heavy weight of responsibility. He didn't dare be reckless. Too much depended on his success.

He had no trouble finding the trail. He found a couple of spots of blood, found too where the wounded outlaw had mounted behind the other one.

He took the trail cautiously. He expected no ambush immediately, but he didn't underestimate either of the men he was following. They had been wanted for a long time and they had not been caught. That, in itself, was evidence that they both were smart. They might do the unexpected simply because it was unexpected.

At first, the trail led straight upcountry. After half a mile, it came to the winding, dusty, two-track road, and followed it for about another mile. The two men had been heading straight for home, Dunbar realized. They had changed their minds after traveling a mile and a half, and having time to think, they had realized going home would be the most foolish thing that they could do. It would identify them, beyond any doubt.

The trail suddenly left the road, and now

it began to wander. It climbed ridges, descended into ravines. It crossed dry washes, angled across rocky slopes, sought out patches of scrubby cedar and piñon pine.

Dunbar followed it slavishly for about three miles. Then he stopped. He realized what the pair was doing. They were leading him back and forth, using up his time. They were leading him into and out of half a hundred likely ambush sites, all of which he came safely through. They were trying to make him careless and when he had become careless, they'd catch him in an ambush he didn't expect because the spot would be such an unlikely one. Dunbar had been hunting men for nearly seven years. He knew the workings of their minds.

He stopped, frowning. He had three choices. He could continue to follow trail, hoping he could spot their ambush before they cut him down. Or he could leave the trail and go straight to their shack up the road from Daisy's place. The trouble with that course was that it was almost as dangerous as the first. They'd be hidden, if they were at home, and he would be exposed.

The third alternative was the one he chose because it was the only one of the three that would put him on equal terms with them. He would return to town. They had sought him out once and would again. They couldn't afford to let him leave and if he stayed they couldn't afford to let him live.

With his decision made, he turned his horse and headed back toward town. He wondered if the two men had watched him turn back, but he did not look around.

He reached town in late afternoon. He went to the saloon first and ordered beer.

He noticed the bartender looking at the dried blood on the shoulder of his shirt. Nor was the bartender the only one who looked at it.

He drank two beers and then crossed the street to the hotel. He went up to his room and sat down in a chair by the open window. He stared down in the street.

He doubted if he'd see them when they came. But even if he did not, this was the coolest place in the room.

Chapter 10

Grady Morse watched the bounty hunter appear on their back trail, only a dot at first that appeared, disappeared, then reappeared again. He had set the ambush several miles from the Elbert house, knowing that at that distance shots could not be heard by Daisy and her son.

Huett, beside him, murmured, "This time we'll get the son-of-a-bitch."

Morse said, "He ain't dead yet."

This seemed supiciously easy to him. Last night he'd thought they had Dunbar bottled up, that they'd get him when he tried to escape from the Elbert house. But it hadn't turned out that way. They were out a horse,

Huett had a wounded arm, and Dunbar was still on their trail.

Morse had taken a position in some reddish rocks about fifty feet away from the trail where Dunbar would have to pass. Huett was ten or fifteen feet away, also hidden. Now he told Huett, "Get your sights on him when he rides by but don't shoot until I do." He didn't want Huett to shoot prematurely and thus throw his own aim off.

Dunbar was now less than half a mile away. Excitement touched Morse. This time they would get the man. After that, they'd take his body down to the Elbert place. It was too bad to have to get rid of Daisy and her son but it could not be helped. Both of them knew who had ambushed Dunbar yesterday, and therefore knew Morse and Huett were wanted by the law and why.

Morse jacked a cartridge into the chamber of his rifle. Huett followed suit. Morse got himself into a comfortable position, resting his rifle on the rock behind which he was hidden. He didn't see how he could miss.

Dunbar came into sight, climbing his horse out of a gully about a quarter mile away. Suddenly he stopped. He stared ahead in the direction the trail went for what seemed like a long, long time. Morse breathed, "Come on. Come on, you son-of-a-bitch!''

Huett called softly, "What's the matter with him? Why did he stop?''

Morse knew why Dunbar had stopped. He had smelled an ambush. Some instinct had told him it was close. Suddenly Dunbar turned his horse, kicked him into a trot and went back in the direction from which he had come.

Morse cursed. Huett said, "How the hell did he know? He wasn't close enough to see anything.''

Morse said, "He knew. He's been trackin' men so long he can listen to 'em think.''

"What are we going to do?''

"Go home for now.''

"Why don't we just go after him? Two of us ought to be able to kill one no matter how tough he is.''

"Like we did last night?''

"Dark is different. Hell, we couldn't even see to shoot.''

"He could. He got one of our horses and got you in the arm. If it had been daylight, you'd be dead instead of hurt.''

"I still say . . .''

"Ah, shut up. Come on, let's go home.''

Morse walked back to where the horses were tied out of sight. He mounted and headed upcountry toward home. Huett followed sullenly a dozen yards behind.

Morse was beginning to develop a healthy respect for the bounty man. Dunbar had all the instincts of an animal. There was no way, at least no explainable way he could have known the ambush was waiting for him back there. Yet he had known.

There was a sudden, small chill in Morse's spine. Angrily he told himself he was a fool. Dunbar was only a man. But the chill did not go away. It was as if some instinct of his own was telling him the deadly danger he was in. Or maybe it was premonition.

He kicked his horse into a lope, despite the heat. The movement seemed to calm him. Frowning, he tried to think of some way they could get Dunbar without too much risk to themselves.

They reached home. Morse unsaddled his horse and turned him out. Huett put his into the corral to use to catch fresh horses tomorrow and turned the one out that was already there.

Huett went into the house and started a fire in the stove. Morse sat down on a bench before the door, rifle across his knees. He didn't think Dunbar would just ride up and try shooting it out with them, but he wasn't taking any chances. Not with Dunbar.

Huett called, "Want a drink?"

Morse said, "Huh uh." He was trying to think of some way to get rid of Dunbar and he knew whiskey would dull his mind.

He could hear the sounds Huett made in the shack as he prepared supper. The sun sank behind the western hills and dusk came down over the land. Smoke curled up from the chimney and drifted across the bare clearing to the edge of it.

What had Dunbar been doing at the Elbert place? That puzzled him. Did he know Daisy Elbert from someplace else? Was he related to her? Or did he just know her husband?

He decided that he ought to know what Dunbar's relationship was with Daisy before he attempted to decide how best to get at the man. At dawn, he thought, he'd ride down to the Elbert place and talk to her.

After making that decision he tried to relax. He went in and got a drink, and afterward sat down and ate the supper Huett had prepared. He washed the dishes and put them away. As soon as he had finished, he took off his boots, pants, and shirt and got into his bunk.

Huett asked. "You think one of us ought to keep watch?"

"It ain't a bad idea. You call me about midnight and I'll take it from there."

He thought about Dunbar for a few moments more before he went to sleep. He wasn't often scared. A man who lives constantly with danger soon dulls that particular sense.

But Dunbar scared him. Maybe, he thought, they ought to just get the hell out of the country and find some other place to go. He decided against it. Dunbar would follow them. They'd never know when he was going to show up. Thinking that, he finally went to sleep.

Morse and Huett left for the Elbert place at dawn. Morse wanted to arrive and be gone again before the bounty hunter could get there from town.

The sun was just poking its rim above the horizon when they rode into the yard. Luke had apparently gone to fetch the cow, because Daisy Elbert came to the door alone. She was carrying her gun and there was both hostility and suspicion in her eyes.

Grady dismounted and took off his hat. "Mornin', ma'am. We come on the carcass of a horse about a mile from here and we

108

figured we'd better stop by and see if everything was all right."

A shadow of doubt touched her face. Morse said, "Are you all right, ma'am? What happened to the horse? How come he was shot?"

She said, "You ought to know. You're the ones that shot him."

"Us? Why would we be shootin' a horse, ma'am?"

There was more doubt in her eyes. "Didn't you?"

"Course we didn't, ma'am. We weren't nowhere near here yesterday."

"It happened the day before."

He looked down at her sympathetically. "It ain't none of my business, ma'am, but if you want to tell me . . ."

"A man came out from town and while he was here somebody started shooting at the house. They killed his horse and broke most of my dishes . . ."

"He wasn't hurt, was he, ma'am? Or you, or Luke?"

"Nobody was hurt. I thought it was you and Mr. Huett doing the shooting. It sounded like your voice yelling at him to come out."

He laughed. "Wasn't us. I reckon when

somebody's yellin', most voices sound the same."

Some uncertainty still remained in her eyes. Morse said, "Was the man anybody we know?"

"No. He was a stranger."

"Friend of your husband's, ma'am?"

"No." She did not elaborate.

There was still some hostility in her. He said, "But he knew your husband, didn't he?"

She started to shake her head, then stopped. She said, "I don't suppose you'll be satisfied until I tell you, even though it's not your business. The man whose horse was shot is a bounty hunter. He killed my husband and he brought some of my husband's personal effects home to me."

Morse studied her suspiciously. "Now why would a bounty hunter do a thing like that?"

She was losing patience with his prying. She answered the question as though it was the last she intended to answer for him. "His conscience was troubling him. He thought maybe he shouldn't have fired when he did."

Morse asked, "Is he coming back?"

A faint flush touched Daisy Elbert's cheeks. "I haven't the slightest idea, Mr.

Morse. But I would doubt that we'd ever see him again."

Grady Morse nodded, put on his hat and mounted his horse. He said, "Any time we can help you out, Miz. Elbert, you just let us know."

He could tell that she still thought he and Huett had been the ones shooting at the house day before yesterday, but she wasn't absolutely sure. He rode away, the germ of an idea beginning to grow in his mind. Hidden by high brush a quarter mile away, he stopped. He could faintly hear the tinkling of the cowbell around the neck of the Elbert cow. He said, "Wait for me, Ed. I want to have a talk with that boy."

Huett nodded. Morse rode away, heading for the sound of the bell. He came upon Luke driving the cow toward home before he had gone three hundred yards. He halted his horse and said, "Howdy, Luke."

Luke looked scared, as if he was going to run. Morse said, "No call to be scared of me, Luke. I ain't going to hurt you."

"What do you want?"

"Just to talk."

"About what?"

"That man who was at your house yesterday."

"What about him?"

"Don't you know?" Morse looked regretful. "I reckon I've said too much." He turned his horse and started to ride away. Luke called, "Mr. Morse."

He turned his head. "What?"

"What was you goin' to say? About that man?"

"I don't know whether I ought to tell you or not, seein' how your ma seems to feel about him."

"I can ask her."

Morse rode back to the boy. "Maybe I ought to tell you before he ends up takin' your pa's place. He's the one that killed your pa, Luke. Did it for money. Did it for a lousy bounty that was on your daddy's head."

Luke's face lost color. His eyes suddenly looked stricken. He said, "That there's a lie."

Morse said patiently, "You think it is? What you reckon that man's doing here? He didn't know your ma or you before he came, did he? Truth is, he brought your ma a few things that was in your pa's pockets when he killed him."

Luke turned as if to run home and confront his mother with what he just had heard. Morse said, "Wait!"

Luke stopped. Morse said, "Your ma's goin' soft on that bounty man. If I was you I'd keep what I just told you to yourself."

Luke stopped. Morse studied his face. He said, "I just figured maybe your pa would want his son to get even with the man that gunned him down. I reckon he ain't going to rest easy in his grave until that bounty man is dead."

Luke was white. His knees were shaking. Morse said softly, "Take the cow on home, son. Act just like everything was all right. But when that bounty man comes back, you see if you can't put a bullet into him. I figure your pa would expect that much of you."

He turned his horse and rode away. Before he went out of earshot, though, he turned. "Careful how you do it, boy. That man will kill you just as quick as he would a man if he knows what you're goin' to do."

Luke didn't answer. Morse rode back toward the place he had left Huett. He was smiling faintly. Now all they had to do was keep an eye on the Elbert place. Luke would kill the bounty man. When he had done so, the two of them would move in and kill both Luke and his mother with the bounty hunter's gun. And that would be the end of it.

Chapter 11

Luke was numb as he drove the cow toward the house. He didn't see the cow and he didn't see the house. All he could think was that Dunbar had killed his pa, murdered him for the bounty on him. And then he'd come here, to soft soap his ma and make up to him like . . . Luke felt a burning behind his eyes as if he was going to cry. He clenched his jaws and made his hands into fists. The burning finally went away. He suddenly realized he was standing at the edge of the yard. The cow had gone to her accustomed place beside the corral and was now looking back at him as if wondering why he didn't come and milk her the way he always did.

Luke shook himself. He became aware that his mother was also watching him from the doorway. He went that way, ducked his head as he passed her and got the milk bucket. Still without looking at her, he went past her and out the door again. She said, "Luke?"

He stopped without turning. "What?"

"What's the matter with you?"

"Nothin'. I'm just goin' to milk."

"You sick or something?"

"Huh uh." He walked away. He tied the cow to the corral fence, got the one-legged milking stool and sat down to milk.

The familiar rhythm and the sound of the milk squirting into the pail had a soothing effect and the shock of what he had been told began slowly to wear off. For the first time he wondered if Grady Morse had told him the truth.

He didn't wonder long, because it added up. Why, unless Dunbar *was* a bounty man, had Morse and Huett tried to kill him the other day? Morse and Huett must also be wanted men and Luke already knew his pa had been wanted. His mother had told him that much when the news had come about his death. She hadn't told him what his father had done, only that he had been wanted by the law and had been killed resisting arrest.

His mother had been careful how she told him that. She plainly hadn't wanted him to think badly of his pa, yet she'd felt too that he was entitled to the truth about how his father died.

The trouble was, Luke had thought his pa had been killed by a real lawman. To discover that he had been killed for money was something else. That made his killer a murderer.

Dead or alive. Hunted down like an animal. And the money paid to his killer as if he was some kind of hero that deserved pay for what he'd done. But even that was not the worst. The worst was the man coming here, sitting down at their table with them, making over his mother until she seemed to have forgotten what he'd done. Luke thought fiercely, "Damn him! God damn him!" and he knew he would do what Morse had told him to.

The main thing, though, was to act natural. He shouldn't let his mother suspect what he meant to do. Already she had noticed the change in him.

He realized that the cow was dry and that he was still milking her dry teats. He got up, tossed the stool against the corral, and set the bucket carefully aside. He untied the rope and let the cow wander away.

He forced himself to act natural when he carried the milk into the house. He put it down, conscious of his mother's eyes on him. He ducked back out, went to the tank at the base of the windmill and washed. He dried himself, hating to go back into the house but knowing that he must.

His mother *must* know what Dunbar had done, he thought. She had to know. There had to have been some kind of explanation of why he had come. Why, then, if she knew, was she so willing to forgive? How *could* she forgive?

He went back into the house. He forced himself to look at his mother as he did. She looked back at him, seeming to flinch at something she saw in his eyes. She quickly looked away, was silent a moment and then she said firmly, "Luke, I want to know what is the matter with you."

"Ain't nothing the matter with me. Ain't nothing."

"Luke . . ."

Suddenly he couldn't stand it any more. He screeched, "Ain't nothing, I said! Ain't nothing the matter with me! Now let me alone, will you? Let me alone!'' He was close to tears, close to breaking down and he didn't want to do that. If he did she'd probably worm what had happened out of him and then he'd get no chance to kill his father's murderer. He ran out the door, away into the brush. She came after him for a little ways, then, knowing she couldn't possibly overtake him if he didn't want her to, slowly returned to the house, her eyes troubled.

She wondered if Luke could have found out that Dunbar had killed his father. That would explain his strange behavior. And only Huett or Morse could or would have told him that.

Still troubled, she finished preparing supper. Luke hadn't come back so finally she set his food on the back of the stove to keep it warm and went ahead and ate. The sky turned dark, so she lighted the lamp. She waited uneasily, staring at the door.

Maybe she'd been wrong in telling Luke anything about the way his father had died, but she had known he'd have found out sooner or later. Things like that have a way of getting around, and if he'd heard it at school in town it would have been a much greater shock to him.

She thought about Dunbar, remembering him, his face, the strength and steadiness of his eyes. He had killed Frank, for money, and she ought to hate him, but she did not. Frank had been like a stranger. He had been an outlaw and if Dunbar hadn't killed him someone else would have.

All the time she'd been married to Frank, she had turned other men away. But now Frank was dead and she suddenly realized how desperately lonely she had been for the last five years. She didn't have to turn Dunbar away.

Slowly she shook her head, almost unconsciously. It wouldn't work. It couldn't work. Dunbar had killed Frank and even if she could forgive him for it, Luke never would.

The evening dragged. Luke did not return. Several times she went to the door and called but he did not reply. More and more she felt sure he had found out that Dunbar had killed his father and why. He must be out there right now at the edge of the clearing, waiting for her to go to bed, so finally she did. If he would go to such lengths to avoid talking to her, then she supposed she ought to let him alone.

She blew out the lamp and lay in bed wide

awake. After about half an hour she heard Luke come in and go to bed. She pretended to be asleep.

She slept very little that night. She felt desperately sorry for Luke and wished that she could help. The trouble was, she didn't know what to say. Luke was only a little more than nine years old. He was sturdy and self-reliant and sometimes he not only did the work of a man, he acted like a man. He was old beyond his years and she regretted his lost childhood. If only his father had been half the man his son already was . . .

Once she thought she heard him crying, his face buried in the pillow so she wouldn't hear. She ached to go to him but instinctively she knew that doing so would only make things worse. She was glad to see the dawn.

Luke got up immediately, as he always did. He took the milk pail and carried it outside. He went searching for the cow.

Daisy got up and dressed. She combed her hair and put some deer meat on the stove to cook. She sliced some potatoes and put them into the fry pan with the meat. She made coffee and then sat down to wait. Finally she heard the cowbell in the distance.

Luke drove the cow into the yard. He sat down and milked. Then he turned the cow loose and brought the milk to the house.

His face was pale and his eyes told her he had slept no more last night than she. He looked straight at her, almost defiantly, before he put the milk down and went outside again.

The morning was like most other mornings. Luke worked at repairing the windmill discharge pipe, occasionally looking toward town. Daisy did a wash and took it out when it was finished to hang it up. Luke went into the house briefly. She didn't see him come out again because she was behind the line of clothes. When she returned to the house, he was back working on the windmill. She gave no thought to his trip to the house, supposing he had gone in after some tool or other.

They ate warmed-over meat and potatoes for dinner. They were finishing when Dunbar rode up and swung down from his horse.

Luke left immediately, running past Dunbar at the door without either speaking or looking at him. Dunbar asked, "What's the matter with him?"

Daisy shook her head. "I don't know but I suspect Grady Morse or Ed Huett might have talked to him last night. I think Luke knows you killed his father for the price that was on his head."

For several moments Dunbar was silent. Then he said, "I'm sorry that happened. I had kind of hoped . . . Well, I like Luke. I thought maybe we could be friends but now I reckon it's impossible."

She said, "I'll talk to him."

He said, "It won't do any good."

"He knew his father was an outlaw. I told him that when the news came that Frank had been killed."

Dunbar said, "I reckon he could live with that because there wasn't nobody he could blame. Now there is. But he'll get over it after I've been gone a while."

Daisy said helplessly, "I'm sorry."

"So am I."

There were other things Daisy would have liked to say because her first opinion of Dunbar had changed. She could tell from Dunbar's eyes that he also wanted to speak but he did not. He turned toward the door. "I've still got to catch Huett and Morse. I was going to let them come to me but it looks like that will take too long, so I'm going after them. I may not see you again."

She said, "Goodbye." She didn't want him to go and it must have shown on her face because he took a step toward her. Then, suddenly, he whirled and plunged through the doorway.

For the barest instant she thought he had stumbled. Then the report came, flat and wicked, and close on its heels came the horror that was the truth. Luke had shot Dunbar. He had killed him and she realized, too late, that this must be what Morse told him to do last night when he talked to him. Avenge your father by killing the bounty man. She was running, out through the open door. She threw herself down beside Dunbar, deliberately placing her body between him and Luke who stood by the windmill with the smoking gun in his hands. It was only a single shot, but it could be reloaded and fired again in very little time.

Luke was white-faced, frozen where he stood. She caught that one quick glimpse of his face. Then she turned her attention to the man on the ground.

Relief flooded her when she saw that he wasn't dead. His face twisted with pain, he said, "The little booger shot me!" as if he couldn't believe it was possible.

"Where are you hurt?"

"Leg." He sat up and put both hands to his leg where blood oozed from a hole in his thigh.

"Let me help you inside."

"You get that youngster's gun before you do anything."

She got up, went to Luke and took the gun out of his hands. She opened the trapdoor action to make sure he hadn't loaded it again. The spent cartridge dropped out and smoke curled up from the chamber of the gun.

She wanted to say something to Luke, but right now there were more important things. She hurried to the house, put the gun inside, then returned to Dunbar, who was trying to get up. She helped him, and he leaned on her, and together they staggered inside. He sank quickly into a chair, the wounded leg stretched out straight in front of him.

Daisy got a knife to slit his pants and underwear and expose the wound. She got bandages and water and whiskey and returned to him. He was sweating and pale but he gritted his teeth and said, "You just leave that stuff with me. I can manage fine. Right now that boy needs you a sight more than I do."

For a moment she stared at him. He had begun to make the slit in his pants leg longer with the knife.

Her eyes flooded with tears. She turned and ran out the door. She ran straight to Luke, dropped to her knees and took the sobbing boy into her arms.

Chapter 12

There was a small hole where the bullet had gone in, bluish around the edges and oozing blood. Fortunately the bullet had missed the leg bone, but it had left a ragged hole larger than a silver dollar where it had come out. Blood flowed freely from the exit wound.

He picked up the brown-glass whiskey bottle and pulled the cork. He took a drink, waited a moment, then took another one. He waited, took a third, then sat there for the whiskey to take effect. Blood dripped from his leg onto the floor.

He began to feel the effects of the whiskey after a few minutes and when he did, he poured some onto the wound, both front and back. Pain like that of a red-hot iron immediately shot through his leg. He quickly corked the bottle, put it down, and steadied himself by holding onto the sides of the chair.

Gradually the pain subsided. He reached for the bandages Daisy had left for him. They were simply strips torn from some kind of cloth. He made a pad and laid it over the exit wound. Then he began to wind bandages around his leg to hold it in place. He was careful not to wind them too tightly. Blood soaked the bandage before he had finished, but he knew that the bleeding would eventually stop of its own accord. No artery had been cut.

He tied the strips and reached again for the whiskey bottle. Daisy came in the door. Dunbar asked, "Is he all right?"

"I don't know." There were tear streaks on her face. She said shakily, "He's only a little boy. How could he . . . ?"

"Where is he now?"

"He ran away into the brush. I couldn't catch up with him."

Dunbar said, "I'll leave. I'm sorry for what's happened. I won't come back again."

"You can't leave. Your leg . . ."

"I can ride if you'll help me on my horse."

"What will you do?"

"Go after Huett and Morse."

She looked at him exasperatedly. "Can't you just forget them and go away?"

He shook his head.

She said stubbornly, "Then you need to rest. You need to give that wound a chance to heal. How do you expect to take two perfectly able men when you can hardly hobble to your horse?"

He didn't answer because he didn't know himself. He forced himself to rise. His head whirled and he stood there swaying. Daisy came to him and steadied him. "You can't go. You've got to stay."

He shook his head. "I've caused enough trouble as it is. The sooner I leave the sooner Luke can begin getting over this."

She said, "Please . . ."

Harshly he said, "Damn it, woman, I ain't going to stay!"

Her face flushed. He headed toward the door and she stayed beside him, supporting him.

His horse danced away, frightened by the smell of blood. Speaking soothingly, Dunbar caught him. It was his right leg that was hurt, so he was able to mount. But the effort made lights flash before his eyes and made his head whirl crazily.

He looked down at Daisy Elbert's face. Her eyes showed a mixture of pity for the pain he was in and exasperation at his stubbornness. He said, "I wish it could have ended differently."

She nodded soberly, her eyes meeting his unflinchingly.

He said, "Goodbye."

"Goodbye."

He turned the horse and crossed the little clearing at a walk. He glanced back once, seeing Daisy standing there looking after him. He had the feeling she was crying but he was too far away to be sure. He caught movement in the brush at the edge of the yard and saw Luke there, watching like some wild thing.

He forced himself to put them both out of his mind. If he was going to stay alive for the next twelve hours it was going to take every bit of concentration and willpower he possessed. He was weak and in pain and his mind was not too clear. In spite of that, he had to either capture or kill both Huett and Morse.

Angling right, he put his horse up the

slope at the side of the valley. The horse lunged upward, with Dunbar hanging onto the saddle horn with both his hands. He was unable to put any weight on the wounded leg, so it would have been impossible to stay in the saddle without holding on.

High enough to see the length of the valley for half a dozen miles he stopped his horse. He was sweating, but his skin felt clammy and cold. Resting in the saddle, he stared up and down the valley, looking for movement or dust. He could see Daisy Elbert's place, with its windmill, its barn, and its corral, but he could see no movement in the yard. Looking upcountry, he couldn't yet see Morse's place. Nor could he see movement of any kind.

Paralleling the slope, he rode slowly north. He felt drowsy now, and fought constantly to stay alert. It was the whiskey, combined with the loss of blood.

Twice he dozed, both times snapping awake with a feeling of panic running through him. Both times the horse was plodding placidly along, threading his way between gnarled cedars and piñon pines. Two hours after leaving the Elbert place, Dunbar sighted Morse's adobe shack ahead, recognizing it from the description of it

Daisy Elbert had given him.

He halted immediately. He didn't dismount; he didn't dare. If he did, he knew it was possible he wouldn't be able to mount again. Weakness was increasing in him and all he wanted now was to lie down and sleep.

From behind a thick piñon pine, he stared at the little shack for a long, long time. No smoke rose from the chimney. There was no movement in the yard. The door was closed and no horses stood saddled in the yard. There *was* a horse in the corral, though, standing with his head down, idly switching his tail at flies.

Dunbar finally decided that Huett and Morse were gone. But the single horse in the corral made him uneasy enough to make him circle wide and come upon the shack from a blind side, where there was neither a window nor a door. Reaching the wall, he dismounted heavily, clinging to the saddle horn for a full minute afterward waiting for his head to stop spinning.

He eased his rifle from the saddle boot and as quietly as possible jacked a cartridge in. He hobbled toward the front corner of the house, leaving his horse ground tied.

He stopped again. He caught himself thinking of bed, and of closing his eyes and letting himself sink into oblivion. He shook his head to clear these thoughts from it. He'd sink into oblivion all right if he didn't stay alert. Either Morse or Huett or both of them might be inside the shack. They might be taking an afternoon nap or playing cards.

He waited for what seemed an eternity, listening. Finally he reached up and thumped his rifle barrel against one of the rafters. No answering sound came from within the shack. Satisfied at last, Dunbar hobbled to the door and opened it, rifle cocked and poked ahead of him. It was gloomy and dark inside, but no one was there.

Dunbar leaned his rifle against the wall inside the door and went around the corner to his horse. Hobbling painfully, he led the animal to the dry wash behind the house. He found a place he could descend into it and did so. He walked along the bottom until he found a protruding greasewood root to which he could tie his horse. He returned, climbed out of the wash and went back to the cabin. He picked his rifle up, went inside and closed the door.

It was stuffy and very hot. Flies droned against the dirty window pane. Dunbar stared at the rumpled, unmade bunks at the rear of the single room. He knew he had to have some rest. He'd have to take a chance and hope he'd awaken when the two returned.

There was a rickety washstand holding a water bucket, dipper, and washbasin. He pulled it over in front of the door and positioned it so that it would topple with a crash if anybody opened the door. He laid down on the bunk, his cocked rifle resting on his chest with its muzzle toward the door. He closed his eyes.

It seemed only an instant before he snapped awake. His hand tightened on his rifle. Its muzzle was still pointed at the door.

He realized immediately that he had slept for quite a while. Sunlight slanted into the window at an angle that told him the sun was about to set. He lay still for several moments, listening. He heard nothing, so he finally eased himself to a sitting position. He put his feet carefully on the floor.

His leg pained ferociously, but his head was clear. He got up, moved the washstand away from the door and opened it. He looked outside. The area around the cabin was as deserted as it had been when he arrived.

Dunbar went back and sat down on the

edge of the lower bunk. He frowned. He couldn't understand where Morse and Huett were. He doubted if they'd have gone to town. He didn't believe they'd leave the country, although it was possible.

He moved the washstand back in front of the door. He lay down again on the bunk. He tried to stay awake, but it was impossible. The wound had taken too great a toll of his strength.

He slept again, and did not awake until dawn had grayed the sky. This time he sat up quickly, genuinely alarmed.

There could be only two possible reasons why Huett and Morse had not returned. One was that they had left the country for good rather than face the chance that he would kill or capture them. The other was that they had gone to Daisy Elbert's place. With Daisy and her son as hostages, they could force him to do anything they told him to.

He left the cabin and hobbled to where he'd left his horse. Briefly he felt bad about leaving the animal tied all night. But he could feed and water the horse later on today.

He mounted with difficulty and headed south toward the Elbert place. He traveled at a walk because he couldn't stand the pain of any other gait. But a terrible urgency was prodding him. Daisy and her son had suffered enough on his account.

Chapter 13

From the brush at the edge of the clearing, Luke Elbert watched Dunbar ride away. He could see his mother standing in front of the door, watching too. Dunbar disappeared into the high brush and Luke felt a sudden sense of loss. He had liked Dunbar. He had felt irresistibly drawn to the man. And now he had shot him. He had hurt him and had driven him away.

His mother turned her face toward him. "Luke?"

He didn't answer.

She called again, seeing him. "Luke, come here. I'm not going to punish you."

He took a hesitant step toward her. She

didn't move and she didn't call to him again. It was like he'd been himself sometimes trying to coax some wild thing to approach. He took another tentative step, and then was clear of the brush. His mother said, "Luke, he's gone. He's not coming back. We can go back to the way things were before he came."

Her saying that should have made him feel good but it did not. He shuffled toward her. He felt ashamed but he couldn't tell her that he did. He felt compelled to defend himself but how do you defend yourself when you have not been accused? She asked, "Did you get the windmill fixed?"

He felt the tears come like a scalding flood. And suddenly he was running toward her, not a man, not a boy who had learned to behave like a man and do man's work, but only a boy. She dropped to her knees and caught him in her arms, and he sobbed without restraint. His body shook and she held him close and began to cry herself because she couldn't help it no matter how she tried.

Luke had needed a father for a long, long time and Dunbar had come and had briefly filled that need, but Luke had shot him and he was gone and nothing now could fill the void or ease the pain. Only time could do that and time has a slow way of healing things.

She held him for a long time, and gradually his sobbing quieted. His pride reasserted itself and he pulled self-consciously away from her and knuckled the tears out of his eyes.

Daisy said, "Mr. Morse put you up to shooting him, didn't he?"

He nodded.

She said, "Mr. Morse is afraid of him. He used you to do what he was afraid to do himself."

He nodded again, knowing this. She said, "Mr. Dunbar has gone after Mr. Morse and Mr. Huett. But he will be all right. He is a strong man and he will be all right."

Luke looked into her eyes. She was saying that Dunbar would be all right but she didn't even believe it herself. She was afraid, and it showed, and he knew he was to blame for Dunbar's danger and his mother's fear. Unwounded, Dunbar might have been a match for Huett and Morse. Wounded, he would probably be killed.

But there was nothing to be done. He would just have to pray and hope his prayers were heard. He headed toward the windmill, feeling a chill in his body even though the day was hot and still.

Daisy went into the house. She felt an overwhelming sense of loss. She had wanted Dunbar to stay. She had wanted him to . . . But it was too late. He might be dead even now. And if he wasn't, he soon would be.

She went about her work almost frantically. Though it was late in the day, she got everything that could be washed and put water on to heat. While it was heating she swept the floor and put the washtub out.

When the water was hot enough, she began to wash, working as hard as she could as if only hard work could still her thoughts, could dull her sense of loss. But it did not.

The sun settled toward the horizon in the west. And suddenly she heard voices in the yard.

She had not heard approaching horses. She looked out, surprised, and saw Morse and Huett sitting their horses looking down at Luke. Hands dripping, she went outside. Morse was grinning as he asked, "You get him, kid? That looks like blood all over the ground in front of the door."

Daisy said, "I killed a chicken," before Luke could reply. She wasn't going to let these two know Dunbar was wounded if it could be helped.

Morse swung down from his horse. "Well, we'll stay for a chicken supper then."

"We had it for dinner at noon."

"Where's the feathers?"

Luke said, "I buried them."

"Buried a few feathers? Where?"

Daisy saw they weren't going to get away with it. She said, "Never mind, Luke. They know."

Morse was grinning. "Where'd you hit him, boy?"

Daisy said, "Leg. It wasn't much." She could see how scared Luke was. She could also see that he thought it was up to him to do something, to make amends. He had an iron wrench in his hand, and suddenly he threw it at Morse. It missed Morse's head and struck him on the shoulder. But it hurt. She could see that in Morse's face.

He reached Luke in a couple of strides and grabbed him by an arm. Luke kicked him in the shin. Daisy screamed, "Luke! Don't!" but it was too late. Luke kicked again and Morse hit him on the side of the head with enough force to send him sprawling in the dirt.

Morse was after him immediately and yanked him to his feet. Daisy rushed at

Morse to keep him from hurting Luke again. Huett slid off his horse and intercepted her. He grabbed her and held her, grinning. He said, "Well, now, looks like I got the best of it."

Daisy bit his hand. He let her go, looked at the bleeding teethmarks in his hand and hit her in the face. The blow struck her partly on the mouth and cut her lip. She tasted blood.

Morse said, "Whoa now. This ain't gettin' us nowheres. Bring her on in the house, Ed. I'll bring the kid. I reckon this is just about as good a place as anywheres to wait for that bounty man. Appears he's soft on these two and he ain't likely to want 'em hurt." He dragged Luke toward the house. Huett let Daisy go by herself but followed close behind, his bleeding hand to his mouth, an angry scowl on his face.

Daisy knew there was no use fighting them. Doing so would only result in even rougher treatment than they already had received. Besides, Dunbar was gone. He had said he would not be back. She said, "He is gone. Luke shot him and he has gone. He is not coming back."

Morse shut the door. He picked up the gun Luke had shot Dunbar with and checked to see if it was unloaded. He put it down again. He said, "He'll be back all right. When he can't find us, he'll know right where to look."

Daisy said, "I've got to hang out the wash."

"Sure. Go ahead. We'll have the kid in here to make sure you don't do nothing you'll be sorry for."

Daisy picked up the heavy tub of clothes. She carried it out the door. There were still clothes hanging on the line from the washing she'd done this morning. She had to take them down to make room to hang the wet ones out. She carried them into the house, then went back out and began to hang the others up. These were things that hadn't really needed to be washed. She'd only washed them to try to quiet her fear.

But she knew that nothing was going to change. Morse and Huett were going to stay here, holding them prisoner, until Dunbar came to look for them. That might take a day. It might take a week. But eventually Dunbar would come because when he didn't find either Morse or Huett he'd know they had either come here or left the country. He'd check this place before he went looking for them someplace else.

Furthermore, Daisy knew that while Huett and Morse needed them now for hostages, they wouldn't need them after they'd taken care of Dunbar. She and Luke would be witnesses against the two and if they intended to stay here, which apparently they did, they'd have to get rid of both her and Luke.

Well, she thought, they weren't dead yet. Something might happen to turn things around. Morse and Huett might not be successful in killing Dunbar when he came. Or she might get a chance to seize one of their guns . . .

She finished hanging up the clothes and returned to the house. The two horses still stood saddled in the yard. Either Morse and Huett wanted Dunbar to know they were here or else they just plain didn't care.

She sat down beside Luke on the bed, but she didn't put her arm around him the way she wanted to. He was scared but he wasn't letting it show and she didn't want to do anything that would make it harder for him. Morse had found the whiskey and was drinking it, occasionally passing the bottle to Huett. Everybody seemed to know it might be a long, long wait.

Riding all the way to the Elbert place was pure torture for Dunbar. His leg and arm both pained him more fiercely even than they had yesterday. Every step the horse took made stabs of pain shoot through his leg. The leg hung loosely because it hurt him too much to put it into the stirrup. And he held the horse to a walk to reduce the movement his leg would be subjected to.

He was weak from loss of blood and from the shock of the constant pain. If Morse and Huett had left the country, and if he had to chase after them, he'd have to take time to let his leg heal up before he went. He'd go to bed in his room at the hotel and he wouldn't get up until he felt like doing so.

But if Morse and Huett *had* gone to the Elbert place, giving his leg a chance to heal would have to wait.

What would he do if they were holding Daisy and Luke hostages? The answer to that one eluded him. Hell, what could he do? He couldn't lay out in the brush and shoot it out with them. If they threatened either Daisy or Luke, he'd have no choice but to give himself up to them. Which would mean his death and afterward the deaths of both Daisy and her son.

Again he wished he'd never come here at

all. He could have sent the money to Daisy and he'd have been reasonably sure of her getting it. He hadn't had to come. But his conscience had been bothering him . . .

Of one thing he was very sure. Morse and Huett were the last fugitives he'd ever run to earth. He was through hunting men.

Staying on the road, he reached the Elbert place in less than two hours, but when he drew near to it, he took to the brush, and when he got close enough for them to see him sitting atop his horse, he dismounted, tied his horse and went on afoot.

He didn't need to get closer than a quarter mile. He saw the three horses in the corral and knew they did not belong to Daisy Elbert and her son. He saw the two saddles on the top rail. He had guessed right. Morse and Huett were here. They were waiting for him to show up.

He took another step toward the small house and stopped. If they didn't know he was here, neither Daisy nor Luke was in any immediate danger. Maybe he could get help. Maybe he could do by guile or stealth what he could not do openly.

He retreated. The sun was about halfway up the sky. He reached his horse and laboriously mounted him. He hesitated for a moment, thinking of how long a ride it was to town. He thought of the way the people there had watched him and looked at him.

Then he remembered the little cabins that had been between here and the adobe shack occupied by Huett and Morse. There had been someone living in one of them, even though the other had looked deserted.

He headed up the road, aware that if he didn't find someone he'd have to go back to town and that he'd be much farther away from it by then.

It was almost noon when he reached the place. He called out and the door opened. A man came out, a big man with black hair and dark skin. Dunbar said, "I'm Ross Dunbar."

The man nodded. "I know. I will not resist. I will go back with you."

Dunbar stared at him. "What the hell are you talking about?" But he knew. This man was wanted, just as Morse and Huett were. Only this one was tired of running and wasn't willing to kill again to remain free. The man opened his mouth to explain but Dunbar cut him short. "Never mind. I don't want to hear."

He stepped down off the horse, holding his weight off his wounded leg by hanging onto the saddle horn until he could put his left foot down. He dropped the horse's reins and hobbled toward the house.

He remembered this man now, remembered his face as being one from a wanted poster he had been carrying. The man's name was Quirino Madrid. He was wanted for murder.

He said, "I could use a drink."

"I have some wine, señor."

Dunbar followed him inside. He accepted a cup of wine and as he sipped it he told Madrid about Morse and Huett holding Daisy Elbert and Luke prisoner. He knew nobody could do anything until it got dark, so when Madrid offered him food he accepted it, knowing he needed it to keep up his strength.

Afterward Madrid suggested that he sleep until just before it got dark. Dunbar started to shake his head but then he stopped. If he was going to stop hunting men then sometime he was going to have to start trusting them again. He nodded and laid down on Madrid's bed. He was almost instantly asleep.

Quirino Madrid stood there staring at the exhausted, sleeping man for a long time.

Finally he stepped outside, closing the door softly behind him.

He had wrestled with his conscience for two days now and he knew it had been much too long. He was intensely relieved that Dunbar had not been killed. If he had, Madrid would have had two killings on his conscience instead of one.

Now, with Dunbar sleeping inside his shack, Madrid knew he was responsible for him. He wouldn't hesitate any more. If Morse and Huett came for Dunbar, he'd fight them off. And when Dunbar came to, if he wanted help, Madrid meant to give it to him.

The killing of Julio Chavez had been unavoidable. He had killed Julio in defense of his own life and should feel no guilt over it. But that killing and the fact that he was a fugitive didn't have to change his character. It didn't have to turn him into an outlaw or a cold-blooded killer like Huett and Morse.

He went back into the shack and got his rifle. He loaded it and got a handful of shells for it off the shelf. He went back outside and sat down in the shade, the rifle across his knees. Dunbar would be safe until he awoke. And when he did, he wouldn't have to go after Huett and Morse alone.

Chapter 14

It was dusk when Dunbar awoke. For several moments he lay still, trying to collect his senses. Then he remembered. He had come to this house to look for help and its occupant had turned out to be Quirino Madrid, a wanted man, whose picture had been on one of the posters stolen from Dunbar's blanket roll.

He had a sudden sinking feeling. Even before he sat up he knew he would be alone. He had slept while Madrid escaped and he'd get no help from him.

A shadow filled the doorway and a voice asked, "Are you awake, señor?"

"Yeah. But I thought you'd be gone."

149

"No, señor. A man tires of running."

Dunbar got up and limped to the door. He stepped outside. His arm ached and his leg still burned like fire. He felt lightheaded and sick at his stomach. Madrid asked, "Would you like something to eat?"

The thought made Dunbar's stomach churn but he knew food would make him feel better.

Madrid went into the cabin and stirred the fire in the stove. He added wood and put on a big covered pot. He lighted a lamp, got the wine bottle and poured a little into two tin cups. He handed Dunbar one of them.

Dunbar sipped it. He looked at Madrid. Bluntly he asked, "Who'd you kill?"

"A man named Julio Chavez."

"Why?"

"A fight, señor. Over a woman."

"Fair fight, or did you murder him?"

"It was a fair fight, señor. The trouble is, Julio's father is the owner of a great Spanish land grant and a man of much influence."

"So you ran away. What happened to the woman? Do you know?"

"No, señor. But I doubt if she was worth having two men fight over her."

"And what will happen if you're taken back?"

"I will be hanged."

"You sure of that?"

"I am very sure, señor."

"Well, I ain't going to take you back. When I get Morse and Huett, I'm through taking anybody back."

"You have been hunting men for a long time, señor?"

"Six years."

"And why did you begin?"

Dunbar could smell the lamb stew on the stove. The wine was warm in his stomach and as long as he was still, the pain in his arm and leg was less. He was surprised to discover that he liked Madrid.

How long had it been since he'd taken the time to like another man? Too long. He said, "My brother and his family were killed for a hundred dollars that he had. I couldn't get the local sheriff to go after them. So I did."

"And you caught them, señor?"

"No. I lost the trail. But I got to wondering how many other killers had gotten away because the law refused to go after them. So I started hunting men that had reward posters out on them."

"And you have since found the men who killed your brother and his family?"

Dunbar shook his head. "Never did.

Likely never will. I don't know their names or even what they look like."

The two were silent a moment. Then Madrid asked, "What will you do after you have finished with Huett and Morse?"

"Go to ranchin', I guess, if they don't get me before I get them. I've got enough to buy a piece of land and put some cattle on it."

Madrid took the stew off the stove and filled two tin plates. At first Dunbar had to force himself to eat, but after eating some he began to feel better. Madrid said, "There was another man—Mitch Harrow. He came to tell me that he had seen my picture on one of the wanted posters you were carrying."

"Then he must be the one that got into my blanket roll."

"And he must have gone on up the road and seen Huett and Morse. But I haven't seen him since."

"Maybe they got rid of him." He thought of Daisy Elbert and of Luke. He finished the stew and got to his feet. "I'd better go. I don't think they'll hurt Mrs. Elbert and her son as long as I'm running loose but I can't be sure."

Madrid said, "I will go with you. You will have no chance if I do not." He got his hat, blew out the lamp and followed Dunbar out to the door. Dunbar's horse had been unsaddled, watered, and fed. He threw the saddle on and cinched it down and Madrid saddled his own animal. Both men mounted and headed down the road in the dark. Madrid asked, "What will you do when you get there, señor?"

Dunbar said, "Try to jump 'em, I guess, if it can be done without getting Mrs. Elbert and her boy killed."

"And if you cannot?"

Dunbar admitted to himself that, as a last resort, he would surrender himself to Huett and Morse. If Daisy and Luke were threatened and if he believed the threat, he would probably give himself up. But maybe it wouldn't come to that.

Holding their horses to a walk, it took more than two hours to reach the Elbert place. A lamp was still burning inside the house but the door was closed and there was no sign of movement. Dunbar and Madrid tied their horses in the brush far enough away so that they'd not smell the horses in the Elbert corral, far enough so that their movements would not be heard. Then the two moved forward cautiously until they found a shallow wash a hundred and fifty yards from the house in which they could conceal themselves.

Dunbar could see the dim shapes of three horses in the corral and knew Morse and Huett were still here. He sat down and put his back to the bank of the wash. He wanted a cigar but he didn't have one and wouldn't have risked lighting it if he had. Madrid said, "What brought you to Dry Creek, señor? Huett and Morse?"

"Huh uh. I'm the one that killed Frank Elbert. I brought the money he had on him to give to his wife."

"Could you not have sent it, señor?"

"Yeah. I could. I told myself I didn't because I was afraid it'd never get to her. Only that wasn't it. Truth was, killin' him bothered me."

"You thought it could have been avoided?"

"Maybe." Now he was wondering something else. How many men like Madrid, unjustly accused, had he captured and taken back, to prison or to be hanged?

He snorted disgustedly. It would serve no useful purpose, going back over them one by one. He'd only torture himself. He wasn't going to hunt men any more and, besides, it was likely that a good many more of those he'd captured were like Morse and Huett than were like Madrid.

The light finally went out at the house. Dunbar said, "One of them would be on guard."

Madrid didn't answer him. Dunbar said, "We'll give the guard time to get drowsy."

"Do you want me to go in with you?"

"Yeah. But don't let 'em know you're around. If something happens to me, maybe you can still get Mrs. Elbert and her boy away from them."

They were silent, waiting. Dunbar figured he ought to give the guard at least an hour to get sleepy before he tried sneaking up on him.

There were two bunks at the rear of Daisy Elbert's cabin. Usually Luke slept in the top one and she slept in the bottom. Tonight, Grady Morse had taken over the bottom one. Luke had offered her his, but she refused. She sat up in a chair, unable to sleep, terrified and wondering what was going to happen to them.

She knew that Dunbar would come eventually. It was inconceivable that he would leave the country without capturing Morse and Huett. They had wounded him twice and he knew what a threat they were to Luke and to her.

Huett was outside, on guard. She supposed he was sitting on the stoop, a rifle across his knees.

If only, she thought, Dunbar wasn't wounded. But with his leg in the shape it was, it would be almost impossible for him to move quietly, almost impossible for him to sneak up on Huett and overcome him.

Furthermore, there was nothing either she or Luke could do to help him when he came because they had no way of knowing when that would be.

Sitting there in the darkness, she examined her own feelings where Dunbar was concerned. She stripped them of all false modesty, of all the pretenses people put forth to hide their true feelings and she admitted that now that she knew what he was really like, she wanted him. She wanted him to marry her and take her away from this place. She wanted him to fill her need and to fill Luke's need as well. Luke would get over the shock he'd felt when Morse had told him Dunbar had killed his father for the bounty on his head. He had liked Dunbar before and he would again. Most important, he would grow up with a man to take his dead father's place, and every boy needed that.

But neither of them would get the chance

if Dunbar was killed when the trap Morse and Huett had set for him was sprung. There had to be *something* she could do.

The room was dark. She could hear Morse snoring softly on the bunk. She didn't know whether Luke was asleep or not. Probably he was not. Probably he was as frightened and nervous as she was.

She considered getting up silently, getting a kitchen knife and plunging it into Morse as he slept. The thought made her chest feel hollow. It made her hands and knees begin to tremble violently.

However much she might want to do it, she realized, she wasn't capable of it. She might be able to use a knife if she was fighting for her life or if she was protecting Luke. But to plunge a knife into a sleeping man cold-bloodedly? No. For her that would be impossible. And if she forced herself she'd bungle it and end up getting killed herself.

What, then, could she do to even up the odds? She might be able to hit Morse on the head, she thought. That wouldn't be killing him. That would only be knocking him unconscious.

What would be the best thing to use? Not the stove poker. That was too long and she wouldn't be able to get a good swing with it because of the upper bunk. A skillet, she decided. The big cast-iron skillet would be best. If she hit Morse's head with the bottom of that, it would knock him out without killing or permanently injuring him.

She got carefully to her feet. She stood there silently for several moments, listening to Morse's snores. They did not change cadence, so she tiptoed toward the stove.

The skillet hung from a peg at one side of the stove. She reached it and carefully took it off its peg. She turned.

Morse grunted and shifted position on the bunk. Luke sat halfway up in bed. She motioned with her free hand for him to lie down again. She couldn't see his face because it was too dark, but apparently he understood. He lay down again.

A careful step at a time, she made it back to her chair. It creaked when she sat down, but Morse continued to snore. Daisy bent and laid the skillet on the floor beside her chair as carefully as she could.

She was ready now, she thought. When she heard a commotion outside, if she did, she'd immediately seize the skillet and attack Morse with it. If Dunbar could handle Huett outside, she'd take care of Morse in here.

She wished she could stop her trembling. She wondered if, when the time for it came, she'd be able to hit Morse with the skillet. She had never done a violent thing in her life and the thought of doing this made a ball of ice grow inside her chest.

Then she thought of what was at stake. Luke's life. And hers. Maybe Dunbar's too. Morse wouldn't hesitate to threaten them both to make Dunbar give himself up. And Morse was capable of killing either Luke or her cold-bloodedly if Dunbar hesitated or refused.

No. She might be scared half to death, but she'd use the skillet when the right time came.

With this battle fought out within herself, she discovered that her knees had stopped trembling. She sat straight and still, waiting. Once or twice she bent and touched the skillet handle to reassure herself that she could seize it instantly when she wanted it. The minutes and the hours passed but she stayed ready and wide-awake.

Chapter 15

Dunbar waited what he judged to be an hour. A thin haze of clouds had drifted across the sky, obscuring most of the stars. But there was a faintly luminescent glow to the cloud cover that made it possible to see objects that were silhouetted against the sky.

At last Dunbar got painfully to his feet, using his rifle as a cane. He said, "Let me get a couple of hundred yards ahead of you. And don't make any noise."

Madrid grunted to indicate he had understood. Dunbar hobbled away, careful to disturb no branches, dislodge no rocks. It was a slow and painful process and once he wondered if he was a fool for letting Madrid come along behind him. Madrid was wanted too and all he'd have to do was yell when Dunbar was almost to whoever was on guard at the Elbert place. That man would kill Dunbar and Madrid would have nothing more to worry about.

He put that disquieting thought out of his head. If he was going to stop being a manhunter he'd have to stop thinking like one. He'd have to start trusting his fellow humans again, however it went against the grain.

Carefully he went forward, testing each step before he put down his weight, testing too with the rifle butt to be sure it made no noise. He cleared the last of the brush and stood with a huge clump of it at his back staring across the clearing toward the house.

There was, indeed, a man sitting on the stoop. He was only a shadowy figure against the darker bulk of the house and Dunbar realized it would be impossible to tell whether he was awake or asleep at least until he was close and visible himself.

He didn't wait any longer but turned and moved on, now paralleling the line of brush that marked the clearing. He didn't stop again until he was hidden from the guard on the stoop by the house itself.

Now he turned toward the house, still carefully testing each step before putting all his weight down upon that foot. He was in the clear, and would be visible from the window facing this way, but he figured whichever one of the pair that was not on guard was probably asleep.

It seemed to take forever to reach the house although it could not have taken more than a few minutes at the most. At last he stood beside it, and leaned his weight against it to take the strain off his wounded leg.

Pain was constant now, seeming to shoot upward from his leg all the way to his brain. By comparison, the pain in his wounded arm was nothing. His head whirled and things seemed to tip crazily before his eyes and he thought, Oh God, don't let me pass out now!

He waited, resting for as long as he dared. He knew he couldn't wait too long or Madrid might get too close to the guard and be seen by him. Moving like a shadow but limping heavily and using his rifle as a cane, he approached the corner of the house.

Reaching it, he took time to scan the yard before he peered around. He did not see Madrid. The guard, whoever he was, was sitting on the stoop, rifle held across his knees. He was resting his back against the doorjamb and his head lolled slightly to one side.

Dozing, Dunbar thought. He didn't move immediately but continued to watch the guard. The man's head sank farther and farther to the side. Suddenly he jerked, and straightened up his head. It remained that way for a minute or two, then slowly began to sag again.

Dunbar tensed himself. He knew he'd have to attack swiftly when he did and he prayed silently that his leg would not betray him and dump him on the ground before he reached the guard. If that happened, he'd be killed before he could rise and neither Daisy nor Luke would have a chance.

A faint scuffing sound reached him from across the yard and he knew he didn't dare wait any longer. He rounded the corner silently, moving like a cat stalking a bird, ready at the first movement of his prey to rush.

A step, two, three. He was now almost within reach of the guard. Another step . . .

Suddenly the man's head jerked upright. He straightened, lifting the rifle clear of his knees. He began to turn, trying to bring it to bear.

Dunbar couldn't wait any longer. He had to risk it, to take the chance that his leg would support his weight. Clumsily, more like a bear than a cat, he rushed the remaining distance separating him from the guard. He swung his rifle like a club, holding it by its barrel.

It struck the guard's rifle, which he had brought almost all the way around, and knocked it from his hands. The guard dived for it, and Dunbar clubbed his rifle a second time, aware that the noise would have awakened the other man inside, that he'd either be out here immediately, or would take his vengeance against Daisy or her son.

This time, though, Dunbar's rifle struck the rising man's head before the guard could raise and parry the blow with his own rifle. Striking, it made a sound like a club smashing a melon, and the guard fell away from Dunbar, his form blending with the blackness of the shadows beside the house.

Dunbar knew the man was dead. No one could have survived a skull-shattering blow like that. He turned, reversing the rifle and jacking a cartridge into it. He headed toward the door.

Inside the cabin, Daisy had sat for what

seemed most of the night with the skillet beside her, with her arm hanging and her hand only a couple of inches from its handle. Finally she thought she heard a faint scratching sound at the side of the cabin and tensed. She heard it again and picked the skillet up, resting it on her knees. She was ready to rush toward the bunk, ready to smash Morse in the head with it the moment she heard a commotion out front.

It wasn't long in coming. First there was the sound of sudden movement immediately in front of the door. Then there was the sharp sound of Dunbar's rifle striking Huett's, and, finally, the sound of Huett scrambling for the gun, climaxed by the sound of Dunbar's rifle smashing his skull.

But Daisy hadn't waited beyond the first sounds in front of the door. With the skillet in her hand, she rushed toward the bunk where Morse was sleeping. She raised it over her head, knowing at last that she *could* do this violent thing in defense of her life, of Luke's and of Dunbar's too.

Morse was moving before she could bring the skillet down. He awoke, snatched for his gun, then rolled toward the edge of the bunk.

Daisy brought the skillet smashing down.

But it never struck. Instead it hit the lower rail of the upper bunk, was deflected and its lethal force lost. And she had no time for a second blow. Morse was out of the bunk, swinging his gun with pure defensive reflex.

It struck her on the side of the face with stunning, numbing force. She was flung sideways and crashed against the dish cabinet that had nearly been splintered by bullets a couple of days before. She collapsed at the foot of it amid cascading dishes and glassware, miraculously still conscious but already feeling the blood streaming warm and wet down the side of her face. She put up a hand and it came away sticky with blood.

Morse had swung around to face the door. Suddenly, from behind him, Luke leaped from the top bunk and attacked.

It was all that saved Dunbar's life. Dunbar flung open the door and stood framed in it, silhouetted against the star-glow outside in the yard. Morse raised his gun, clicked the hammer back . . .

Luke hit him at knee level with all his weight and force. It was enough to throw Morse's aim off but not enough to dump him to the floor and make him prey for Dunbar. Luke, furthermore, made it impossible for Dunbar to shoot.

Morse's rifle made an ear-splitting roar in the close confines of the room. The muzzle flash illuminated Dunbar briefly, enough for recognition, and then it faded, leaving Daisy completely and momentarily blind.

Morse swung around. But he didn't strike Luke with the gunbarrel as he had her. If he had, he would have been unprotected and Dunbar would probably have killed him on the spot. Instead he seized the boy, yanked him around in front of him as a shield and roared, "Shoot and you kill this kid, you son-of-a-bitch! Now back off, or by God, I'll kill him myself!"

There was a silence after that. It seemed to last forever but actually could have lasted no more than a couple of seconds at most. Then Dunbar called, "Ma'am? You all right?"

Daisy, knowing Luke was between the two, screeched, "Yes! But don't shoot! He's using Luke . . . !"

She heard the action of Morse's gun and she saw the shadowy figure outside the door dive suddenly to the side. Morse's gun flared again, again illuminating things briefly and again blinding her. But she had seen the empty doorway and knew Dunbar had not been killed.

The door slammed, then, leaving the room completely black. Luke was struggling with Morse and the man impatiently cuffed him on the side of the head and sent him reeling across the room to crash into the stove. Luke collapsed at its foot and didn't move, having apparently struck his head on the heavy, cast-iron stove.

Daisy was suddenly more furious than she had ever been in her life before. All night she had sat with her hand close to the skillet and Dunbar had come just as she had hoped he would. But from then on everything had gone wrong. Now Luke was hurt, as was she, and Morse was still in command of the situation. Dunbar, outside, was as helpless as before.

She seized the first thing that came to hand, a heavy pewter pitcher that had tumbled down from the dish cabinet when she struck its base. She rushed across the room, swinging it, and struck Morse squarely on the nose with it.

He howled with the pain and, as in Luke's case, reacted instinctively. He struck her with his fist, a blow that hit her squarely in the mouth, smashing lips and loosening teeth and sending her staggering back to fall, barely conscious, in the middle of the floor.

Morse cursed savagely, ending the string of curses with, "You goddam she-cat, you come near me again and I'll bust open your stupid head!"

Daisy crawled to where Luke lay unconscious beside the stove. She felt his head, felt the knot that had already raised. It was a vicious wound, and bleeding. But she could feel the rise and fall of Luke's chest.

Crouching there, she shielded Luke's body with her own in case Morse should turn his gun on them. But he did not. He jacked another cartridge in, then stepped to the window and smashed its pane with the muzzle of his rifle. He roared, "Dunbar?"

There was a moment of silence outside the house. Then Dunbar's voice answered, apparently from the corner of the house. "What?"

"Throw down your gun and come on in, or I'll kill the kid and throw him out to you!"

There was silence, longer than before. Daisy thought, No! Don't give up! If you do, he'll kill us all!

Chapter 16

To Daisy it seemed like a nightmare that had no end. Seconds seemed to stretch into hours as she waited for what Dunbar would do. Morse yelled, "Well? Make up your goddam mind!"

Dunbar's voice came back. "Huett's dead. Did you know that? You're all alone in there and the best thing you can do is to give yourself up!"

"Why the hell should I? I'm wanted for murder. I can't get hung but once. A couple more killings ain't going to make no difference!"

Dunbar yelled back, "You're all alone. You ain't going to live long enough to hang.

You're going to be killed by me right here and now."

"By God, I ain't fooling! I'll bash this kid's head in and throw him out!"

There was a moment's silence. Then Daisy heard something that made her doubt her ears. "You think I care? That kid don't mean nothing to me and neither does his ma. Kill 'em both and then I can burn that shack and smoke you out of there!"

Morse left the window and came across the room. "Give me that kid."

Daisy raised up. She tried to fight him off but he cuffed her and sent her reeling across the room again to collapse against the wall. Morse yanked Luke to his feet, limp but beginning to recover consciousness. He dragged him to the window and began slapping his face, trying to bring him back to consciousness. Luke groaned and then began to protest. Morse twisted his arm savagely behind his back and Luke yelled out with pain. Morse bawled, "Hear that? You got about a minute. Then I'm throwin' his body out!"

Daisy, only partly conscious, willed herself to crawl across the floor toward Morse's voice. But she knew she could never make it in time even if she could muster the strength to prevent him from killing Luke when she did get there.

Morse *would* kill Luke, and then he'd kill her. Dunbar, for all his pretending, didn't really care about anything but money. He'd eventually kill Morse and take the two bodies back to wherever they would pay the bounty on them and he probably wouldn't even feel any pangs of regret.

Yet even as she had the thought she didn't believe it in her heart. Still crawling across the floor toward Morse and Luke, she heard Dunbar shout, "All right! I'll make a deal with you! I'll pull back! You get your horse and go! I won't come after you until it's light!"

There was a long silence. Finally Morse yelled, "All right! But no goddam tricks. I'm goin' to hold this kid until I'm ready to ride off!"

There was another wait, while Morse gave Dunbar time to pull back. Then he opened the door. Daisy, still groggy, saw that he held Luke underneath one arm, his rifle in the other hand. He stood there in the doorway for a moment, dimly silhouetted against the starlight outside the cabin, then stepped on out through the doorway and disappeared.

Daisy half expected the immediate sound of a scuffle, or that of a shot, but there was no sound. She got to her feet and staggered to the door. Holding onto the doorjamb to keep from falling, she stared toward the corral.

Morse's shape was dim, barely seen in the darkness. She heard the gate to the corral squeak as it was opened. She couldn't see Luke and wondered where he was. Too groggy yet, perhaps, to try and get away, The blow he'd taken on his head was enough to make him groggy and sick for days.

The horses pounded around the corral and she heard Morse curse angrily. Then, apparently, he got a rope on one and led it to the gate. Morse's shape blended with that of the horse, but she heard the slap of the saddle hitting the horse's back. Shortly after that, the corral gate was flung wide.

Morse stooped to pick something up. Then, heavily, he swung to the horse's back.

The horse trotted away from the corral, across the yard and headed north. For an instant relief flooded Daisy. It was over. Luke, except for the lump on his head, was safe. She was safe and so was Dunbar. Morse would ride away and they'd never see him again.

But as Morse's horse passed the house, she knew, with a hollow feeling in her chest, that she had been wrong. Morse was not alone on the back of his horse. She could make out Luke's limp body thrown across the saddle in front of him. Morse was taking him away.

She pushed away from the doorway and half ran, half stumbled across the yard. The horse saw her, shied, then broke into a lope. He disappeared into the high brush at the clearing's edge.

And Daisy screamed, a long, lost, chilling sound that brought both Dunbar and Madrid to her at a pounding run.

Dunbar knew what had happened the instant he heard Daisy scream. The possibility that Morse might take either Daisy or the boy as hostage had occurred to him, but he had known it was a chance they had to take. Morse *would* have killed Luke and thrown his body out to convince him he would do exactly what he said he would. He'd then have threatened to do the same to Daisy and they'd have had to pull back anyway to save *her* life.

This way, they were really no worse off than they'd been when Morse was inside threatening to kill the boy. At least Daisy was safe. And Morse could be overtaken, if not tomorrow then eventually.

He reached her and she threw herself into his arms, sobbing hysterically. He held her close against him and let her weep, until finally her hysteria began to abate. She wailed, "He's hurt! He isn't even conscious and no telling how bad he's hurt!"

"What did Morse do to him?" Dunbar felt a savage anger growing in his mind.

"Hit him on the head. There was a lump as big as a walnut and there was a lot of blood!"

Dunbar knew Luke might have a fractured skull. At the very least, he had a severe concussion. He said, "Go on in the house and light a lamp."

"A lamp? Aren't you going after him?"

Dunbar said, "Do what you're told! Go light a lamp!" His voice was harsh and stern. For a moment she stood as if frozen. Then she turned and went into the house.

Madrid had come up beside Dunbar. "What now?"

Dunbar said, "There ain't a damn thing we can do in the dark. Hightailin' after him will only wear out the horses and it won't do no good. We'll get a fresh horse in if we can. We'll pack supplies. We'll eat and we'll get what rest we can. We'll be ready to go as soon as it's light enough to trail.''

A match flickered inside the cabin and a moment later the light spread as the lamp wick caught. Madrid asked, ''What about the kid?''

''Well, he's hurt. I don't know how bad. Maybe his head is cracked and maybe it ain't.''

''Will Morse kill him once he figures he's far enough ahead?''

''Might. But don't let her hear you thinkin' that.''

He went into the house. Daisy stared at him coldly, as if he was the enemy. He said, ''We'll need food. Enough to last a week.''

''A week? Luke will be dead by then!''

''Not likely. Luke is pretty tough.''

''But he's hurt.''

''Yes ma'am. He's hurt. But there ain't one damn thing I can do about that. So stop arguing with me and do what I told you to.''

She didn't move. Her mouth was set in a stubborn line and her eyes were hostile and angry. ''I'm going along.''

''No ma'am. You ain't. You'll slow us down and spoil what chance we got of getting Luke away from Morse.''

She folded her arms. ''I'm going along.''

"No."

"You can't stop me. If I can't go with you, I'll follow you."

"Not if I don't catch up a horse for you, you won't."

She looked like a child that has just been slapped in the face. Her eyes filled with tears. Dunbar stared at her a moment. She said, "Please. He's all I've got. I won't slow you down. If I do, you can leave me behind."

He hesitated. Finally he nodded. "All right. Now get the food."

Madrid had gone after their horses. Now he rode into the yard, leading Dunbar's horse. Before he could dismount, Dunbar said, "See if you can find that horse Morse turned out of the corral. If he's with some others bring 'em all in. I'll get started on a grave."

Madrid rode away and it occurred to Dunbar with some surprise that he hadn't thought to doubt the man. He grinned ruefully. He was learning. He walked to the barn and groped around in the darkness until he found a shovel. He came back out, walked to the edge of the clearing and put the shovel down. He went back to the house, got hold of both of Huett's wrists and dragged him to where he'd left the shovel.

He began to dig, an extremely difficult task on account of his wounded leg. He was down half a foot before it even occurred to him that he was burying $750 bounty along with Huett's body. Oddly enough, he didn't seem to care.

Sweating, he paused and leaned on the shovel to rest. His horse stood beside the little cabin with his reins trailing. He could see Daisy Elbert moving back and forth inside, getting food together for the trip.

Madrid came riding in, driving two horses ahead of him. They went into the corral and Madrid closed the gate. Dunbar called to him and Madrid approached. He asked, "What about the bounty?"

Dunbar said, "I told you. I ain't a bounty hunter no more."

"What do you want me to do?"

"Get a lantern at the house. Go out in the barn and see if there's a saddle and packsaddle. Saddle up them two you just brought in. Then ask Mrs. Elbert if she'll fix us something to eat."

Madrid went back to the house. He disappeared inside. He came out with a lantern and a few minutes later Dunbar heard the clatter of the stove lids as Daisy built up the fire. Smoke began to issue from the tin chimney.

Dunbar went back to digging, trying to put out of his mind the disquieting thought that Morse was capable of killing Luke and dumping his body on the trail.

He knew how Daisy would react to that. She'd go to pieces. She'd blame him for bringing all this trouble down on her and Luke and, he admitted, it *was* his fault. If he hadn't come Luke would not now be hurt or in the danger he was in.

Angrily he attacked the ground. He wanted Daisy, wanted her to marry him. He wanted Luke and wanted to be a father to the boy. But only if he was successful in rescuing Luke unhurt would that be possible. If Luke was killed Daisy wouldn't have anything more to do with him.

When he was down a foot and a half he stopped, climbed out of the grave and rolled Huett's body in. He filled the grave without feeling. Huett was a murderer and being killed and buried this way only saved the cost of a public trial and hanging. It also eliminated the possibility that he might escape and kill somebody else.

Finished, he returned the shovel to the

barn, washed at the windmill tank and then limped to the house.

Daisy was cooking venison steaks and sliced potatoes. She turned as he came in, and showed him a face that had regained its composure. "I'm sorry for the way I behaved a while ago."

Dunbar said, "I couldn't blame you. I reckon any mother would have done the same."

"I won't do it again."

Dunbar sat down at the table. After several moments Madrid came in. He took off his hat and flashed Daisy a smile. *"Buenas noches, señora."*

She said, "I think it's *Buenos dias* by now."

Madrid said, "It probably is."

He sat down beside Dunbar and after a few moments Daisy brought the food. She sat down across from them and helped herself after they had helped themselves. They ate in silence. Now and then Dunbar would see a shadow cross her face as she thought of Luke. But she said nothing and he knew she would cause no trouble on the trail.

But he promised himself one thing. If Morse killed Luke, there'd be no place on earth where he could hide. If it took forever, Dunbar would find and kill him or take him in to hang.

Chapter 17

Daisy meticulously did the dishes after they had finished eating. Dunbar and Madrid got the horses ready and loaded the packhorse with blanket rolls and gunny sacks of food. When she had finished in the house, Daisy came out, closing the door firmly behind her as if considering the possibility that she would never return.

There was by now the faintest line of gray in the east. It would be another hour before it would be light enough to trail, but Dunbar knew Daisy's control could stand no more delay. He got the lantern Madrid had used, lighted it and said, "We'll see what we can do by lantern light."

He knew Morse had gone north. Leading his horse and carrying the lantern, he cast back and forth north of the cabin until he picked up the trail. Little could be gained by starting now, a mile at most, but he led out anyway following the trail by lantern light. Daisy and Madrid followed him.

Dunbar had followed a hundred trails in the last six years and he was as expert as any Indian. By the time it was light enough to discard the lantern, he had covered a mile and a half. He turned down the wick, put the lantern down at the side of the trail and mounted his horse.

He glanced at Daisy's face. It was pale, drawn taut, and her eyes were scared. He said, "Don't worry. He needs Luke and he's not likely to do anything to hurt him."

She gave him a wan smile of thanks for the reassurance. Madrid, bringing up the rear, looked at Dunbar as if he thought Dunbar had lied. But Dunbar had spoken in earnest. Morse by now had a healthy respect for him. Luke was the only guarantee he had that Dunbar wouldn't overtake and shoot him down. Luke was his ace in the hole and he wasn't likely to give him up.

The real danger lay in the injury Luke had received last night. If he had a fractured skull, he wouldn't live long no matter how carefully Morse took care of him. If it was only a concussion, a few days would probably take care of it. Rest would hasten his recovery, but he wasn't likely to get much of that.

From the look of the trail, Dunbar guessed that Morse was still five or six hours ahead of them. That didn't worry him. Only a few light clouds floated in the sky. This was arid country, almost a desert, where it seldom rained. The trail wasn't going to get wiped out. They could overtake Morse almost any time they wanted to. But getting him without risking Luke's life was something else.

Morse's trail followed the road until it petered out in the high grass about thirty miles from the town of Dry Creek. After that, it continued on up the canyon toward the distant sandstone rims of a high plateau that, Dunbar knew, stretched almost to the Wyoming line.

In midmorning, he halted the horses to rest them briefly. He dismounted and took his saddle off, then fanned the horse's back with the saddle blanket. Daisy had her saddle off by the time he had finished. He fanned her horse's back a few moments. Then he looked at her.

Her face was still pale. He said, "You've got to quit worrying. It don't do no good. It only hurts you and it don't help Luke."

She tried to smile but it was a forlorn attempt. She said, "I know. That's what I keep telling myself. But I can't seem to stop."

Madrid was rubbing his horse's back with an old gunny sack he carried behind his saddle. He was pretending he couldn't hear. Dunbar said, "I've chased fifty wanted men. Most of them I've caught. I can promise you I won't lose the trail. I can promise you I'll get Luke back."

She nodded and tried to smile again. He didn't know how much he had reassured her but he'd done all he could. Nothing he could say would make her stop torturing herself. Nothing would make her stop worrying.

What troubled Dunbar almost as much as Luke did was his leg wound. The pain was constant and throbbing and he suspected the wound was festering. The shoulder wound was stiff, but less painful than yesterday and he supposed it was probably all right.

After the horses had rested half an hour, they saddled up again, mounted and continued north. The canyon began to narrow as they rode. On both sides, rounded hills rose from the valley floor. Here, greasewood had almost disappeared, replaced by sagebrush, high as a horseman's head on the valley floor, more scrubby on the hillsides rising on both sides of it. Looking ahead, Dunbar could see that there was only one way out. Up, up the trail went as the canyon rose, until at last someplace ahead it would climb through the sandstone rim that rose perpendicularly for a couple of hundred feet.

One thing Dunbar knew. Morse wouldn't be going this way unless he knew of a trail leading out on top. He wouldn't ride into a box canyon from which there was no escape. He had probably come this way a dozen or more times before on his forays out of the canyon with Huett.

At a point he judged was three miles from the canyon's head, they encountered a small stream that sank into the ground in a jumbled pile of rocks. They watered the horses here, then went on. The stream tumbled over rocks in its bed making a pleasant sound. And the trail went on.

At last they reached the end of the canyon. Here, the stream fell from the high rim in a waterfall, rushed down a narrow canyon to the valley floor cutting deeply as it did.

The trail cut to the right here, in switchbacks ascending toward the rim a thousand feet above. Dunbar followed the trail, looking up often to scan the ascending landscape ahead but seeing nothing, no dust, no movement, no specks that might have been a horse or man.

At first the trail followed a narrow gulch that fed into the main canyon. Then the trail climbed out and started across a cedar-covered slope. It left the cedars at an altitude at which they apparently did not thrive and angled up steeply across a slope covered with sagebrush. The tracks of Morse's horse were plain and easy to follow because they followed an established trail, made either by horsemen or by wild game or both. After three switchbacks and about a mile, the trail left the sagebrush and climbed diagonally across loose sandstone that was very soft, very unstable, and which the horses did not like at all. Dunbar's horse tried several times to balk, but he would not permit it, holding the horse's head up and gouging him occasionally with the spurs.

It was here that Morse struck. First indication of it that Dunbar had was a sharp crack from above. Looking up, he saw a cloud of dust and knew immediately what it was. Morse, waiting for them atop the rim, was prying huge pieces off the rimrock with a pole. The crack he had heard was the sound of a boulder striking another boulder and perhaps shattering, thus causing the huge cloud of dust.

The horses, too, had heard the sound. They laid back their ears and rolled their eyes in terror, and like their riders, turned their heads to look upward toward the sound.

The first rock, half as big as one of the horses, came bounding down the slope straight toward them. Dunbar sat frozen, trying to guess what the course of the rock was and where it was going to cross the trail. The guessing was made more difficult by the fact that the rock didn't come toward them on a true course but instead, being squarish in shape, bounded from side to side.

It was still a hundred yards away when Dunbar yanked his terrified horse off the trail so that Daisy could get past and he roared at her, "Ride! The damn thing's coming straight at you!"

He caught a glimpse of Madrid's face. The Mexican was trying to make his horse turn on the narrow trail. The packhorse was also trying to turn, scrambling and fighting the loose, sliding sandstone shale of the slope.

Dunbar heard another sharp crack from above, and another immediately following it. Daisy drummed her feet against her horse's sides. She must have dug heels into his flanks because he suddenly put down his head and began to buck. Daisy sailed off, hit the slope a dozen yards below the trail and began rolling helplessly toward the bottom. Dunbar grabbed for her bucking mount as he went past, but he wasn't close enough to catch the animal.

The first rock, terrifying in its size and in the express-train sound it made, went bounding past, raising a cloud of dust that immediately made everything invisible. Dunbar couldn't see Daisy, or Daisy's horse, or Madrid or the pack animal. He knew he ought to spur ahead and get out of here but he couldn't leave Daisy and he didn't dare dismount from his horse.

He didn't know whether his horse could keep his footing on the shaly slope or not but he had to take the chance. Digging spurs cruelly into the horse's sides, he reined hard over toward the left, literally forcing the horse to leave the trail and plunge down the steep-angled slope. Scrambling, fighting for footing, literally on his haunches, the horse went sliding down the slope, uttering as he did a shrill neigh of terror.

Dunbar stopped worrying about the rocks. If one hit him, then he'd be dead. He'd just have to hope they missed.

Dust was still like a fog, preventing him from seeing more than a few yards ahead. He roared, "Daisy! Where you at? Daisy?"

He thought he heard her muffled cry, ahead and a little to his left. The horse was fighting him now, not wanting to go down but wanting to turn and head back up the slope. Dunbar spurred him savagely, keeping his head inflexibly toward the front. And then, suddenly, he saw Daisy straight ahead.

She had managed to stop her downward rolling progress by spread-eagling herself on the slope and clawing at it with her fingers. She was dusty and scratched and Dunbar didn't know whether he could maneuver his horse close enough to get her up into the saddle with him.

All the time the rocks kept coming, varying in size from three feet in diameter to the size of a man's fist. All bounded rather than rolled, sometimes reaching heights of several feet from the ground.

Dunbar forced his horse to go below where Daisy lay sprawled, then reined him hard around again and spurred him cruelly.

The horse, wanting to go up the slope instead of down anyway, responded quickly. Dunbar, still ten yards below Daisy, roared at her, "You got to get up. Dig in your feet and stand up and grab me as I come past!"

He saw her get to her knees, saw her dig in her feet. She slid a yard or so before she got them deeply enough imbedded, but as he came abreast of her, she got to her feet. He leaned over and she threw her arms around his neck. Her body struck his wounded leg, nearly blinding him with pain, but then he was able to swing her behind him and she got a leg over the horse and took her arms from around his neck and put them around his middle instead.

She was holding on for dear life, but sliding off a little more with each lunge of the horse. Dunbar put his own hand back and got a handful of her skirt and held on.

It seemed forever, but they finally reached the trail. Dunbar turned into it, hearing as he did the sound of a huge boulder striking something yielding behind him on the trail. He knew that either Madrid's horse or the packhorse had been struck. He looked back even as he spurred his horse along the trail, but the dust was so thick he couldn't see anything.

He broke out of the dust cloud and into the open. Both he and Daisy were choking and coughing on the dust. Daisy's horse stood with reins trailing a quarter mile up the trail.

Dunbar continued until he reached her horse. Behind him he could feel her violent trembling. He turned his head and saw that tears were spilling out of her eyes, running across her dusty cheeks and forming little muddy rivers as they did. She was grimy and disheveled but to him she was beautiful because she was alive and safe and even relatively unhurt.

He said, "Easy now. Easy. We're out of it."

"He tried to kill us all!"

"He damn near did it, too." Dunbar was staring back down the trail. He knew that either Madrid or the packhorse was gone, perhaps both of them. He said, "Think you're steady enough to get off and mount your horse?"

"I think so." She slid off on the uphill side and made her way carefully to where her horse stood, still trembling. She picked up the reins and mounted him.

The rocks had stopped coming down. The dust was settling. Suddenly, materializing out of the dust, Dunbar saw Madrid. He kept watching as Madrid approached but the packhorse did not appear.

Silently, to himself, he cursed the loss. It could have been worse because one or more of them might have been killed. But the loss of the packhorse meant they had no food, no blankets, no supplies of any kind. They did not even have water because all the canteens had been on the packhorse.

But there was no use dwelling on the loss. Dunbar motioned to Daisy to go on and the three picked their way upward across the shaly slope.

Chapter 18

At the foot of the rimrock, where the trail
began its ascent up a narrow defile cut by
centuries of water cascading down off the
top of the plateau, Dunbar halted his horse.
He dismounted and Daisy and Madrid
followed suit. Dunbar asked, "Anybody
hurt?"

Madrid fingered a knot on the side of his
head above his ear. "Only this."

Daisy had wrenched a leg so that she
limped when she walked. She was scratched
and cut and her clothes were dusty and torn
in several places, but otherwise she seemed
all right. She asked, "What are we going to
do without supplies?"

Dunbar said, "We'll do without."

"Couldn't we go back and gather up some of them?"

Dunbar shook his head. "The whole works is probably down at the foot of the slope. We'd lose half a day and we might not even find anything usable."

Daisy said, "I wonder where Luke was while he was doing that."

Dunbar said, "Luke got a pretty good rap on the head. He was probably resting while he had the chance."

"You don't think . . . ?"

"No I don't. He's likely sick and groggy but he's still alive." Only he wasn't sure. Morse was capable of hiding Luke's body someplace along the trail well enough so they'd have passed it by.

They rested long enough to let the horses stop their trembling. Then they mounted again and Dunbar led the way up the steep defile and out on top of the plateau.

Up here it was rolling country, in places almost impenetrable because of thick, high, serviceberry brush. Slopes facing north contained thick aspen groves and down along the rims high pines and spruces rose. Madrid called, "Maybe we can get ourselves a deer, señor."

195

"Maybe. We'll watch for one." He was guessing that by now Morse must be an hour and a half ahead of them. He was guessing, further that Morse, having failed to stop them with his rock barrage, might now try to ambush them. If he could kill a couple of their horses he'd probably figure he could make a deal. He'd give Luke up in exchange for them turning around and going back.

Dunbar wouldn't hesitate about doing it, either, if the chance was offered. But as they continued, now heading almost straight east, he reluctantly decided that Morse had no intention of stopping and trying to ambush them. He must have seen the results of the rock barrage. He must have seen their packhorse struck by a rock and knocked rolling down the slope. He knew they were without supplies. If he could stay ahead of them today, and tomorrow, avoiding habitations where they could get supplies, then he knew they would have to go back. Or they'd have to leave his trail and find a town or ranch where they could replenish their supplies.

Morse was obviously pushing his horse just as hard as he dared. All day the trail crossed the high plateau, changing direction only long enough to detour some deep ravine. In late afternoon, it dropped down into a river valley long enough for Morse to water his horse. Afterward it climbed out again, taking to thick timber where there would be no ranches or settlements.

The trouble was, Morse was spooking the game. They hadn't seen a deer all day. At last, near sundown, Dunbar turned his head and spoke to Madrid. "Stay with the trail. I'm going to see if I can't get a deer."

Madrid nodded. He took the lead. Dunbar angled off to the right. By the time he was a half mile from the trail, the sun was beginning to sink behind the horizon.

It disappeared and the few high clouds turned a brilliant orange. They were beginning to fade when Dunbar saw the deer.

The animal, a young spike buck, stood at the edge of a small clearing about a hundred yards away. He was looking at Dunbar's horse curiously but he wasn't yet frightened enough to run. Dunbar knew if he dismounted to get a steady shot, the young buck would be gone.

He raised his rifle slowly. He had fired a gun from his horse's back before. The horse knew what was coming and didn't like it. He laid back his ears.

Dunbar drew him to a halt, knowing that

to shoot from the back of a moving horse gave him little chance of hitting anything. Even the horse's breathing while he was standing still made accuracy difficult. Dunbar waited, holding his aim as steady as he could until the horse had inhaled and was ready to exhale. Then he fired.

The deer leaped high in the air and for an instant Dunbar thought that he had missed. Then the deer crumpled and lay kicking on the ground.

Dunbar rode to him. He dismounted and cut the small buck's throat. Quickly he gutted the animal, saving only the liver out of the deer's entrails. They could eat the liver tonight. He loaded the deer on his horse behind the saddle and tied him in place. Then he mounted and headed back toward Morse's trail.

He caught up with Daisy and Madrid just as it turned full dark. They had halted, had dismounted, and were picketing their horses out.

Dunbar hung the deer carcass in a tree. He staked out his horse and then, by firelight, skinned the deer while Daisy cooked liver on sticks over the fire.

They had no canteens, but had drunk their fill at the stream in late afternoon. They ate the liver and afterward Dunbar had Daisy cook as much of the meat as she could so that they wouldn't have to stop to cook tomorrow.

Once, she looked across the fire at him and said, "He's hurrying. Why?"

"He figures if he can stay ahead of us for a couple or three more days, we'll have to turn around."

"But he must know we could kill a deer for food."

Dunbar nodded. "He does. It ain't the lack of food he's counting on. Or water. It's blankets and slickers. He's headin' straight for the high divide."

"Then what are we going to do?"

"Try catching him before he gets that far." He got up and wandered away from camp, gathering more wood for the fire. Madrid followed him. When they were safely out of Daisy's hearing, Madrid said, "You know he ain't going to be able to keep that boy much longer. The kid weighs close to a hundred pounds. That's going to slow him down."

Dunbar didn't answer. He continued to gather wood. Madrid wandered off in another direction. Dunbar knew Madrid was right. In fact, he thought it possible that

Morse had already gotten rid of Luke.

He wondered how Daisy would take the news that Luke was dead. He was all that she had left. Her husband was dead and he'd never been much good to her even when he was alive. She depended on Luke and needed him. If Luke had been killed, she would blame Dunbar for his death because if Dunbar had never come none of this would have happened and Luke would have stayed alive.

He carried a huge armload of wood back into camp and dumped it on the ground. Frowning and preoccupied, he went after another load. Daisy was still frying meat.

Dunbar brought three more loads of wood into camp. He built another fire about ten feet away from the first. He got the saddle blankets from the three horses and threw them down nearby. They would be all the cover they had tonight, and while they smelled to high heaven, the smell would be better than the cold.

Finally, after Daisy had cooked enough meat to last for at least three days, Dunbar spread it out on some brush to cool and laid down to sleep. Daisy laid down on one side of him and Madrid on the other. The fires died, but they had warmed the ground and unless a strong wind came up, they would probably be comfortable enough.

Dunbar watched Daisy through half-closed eyes. She laid on her back, staring at the sky. He knew she was thinking about Luke and he doubted if she'd get much sleep tonight. At last he said softly, "Tomorrow's going to be a hard day. You need your sleep."

"I know. But I can't go to sleep."

There wasn't much he could say to that. After a while she asked, "Do you think he's still alive?"

"Probably."

She said, "He's extra weight. When Morse starts climbing over the mountains tomorrow . . ."

Dunbar said, "It wouldn't make no sense to kill the boy. He knows if he does I'll stay on his trail until I catch up with him. It'd make more sense to just leave Luke behind. We'd find him and probably go on back. At least that's likely the way Morse is figuring."

Her voice sounded more hopeful. "Do you really think so?"

"Wouldn't say so if I didn't."

She turned silent, then, and after a few minutes her heavy, regular breathing told him she was asleep. But Dunbar didn't sleep. He got up and moved away into the darkness. He sat down and put his back to a rock, the rifle held across his knees. Another option open to Morse was to slip back at night and murder them while they slept. He hadn't mentioned it to Madrid or to Daisy but he had considered it.

He dozed occasionally, feeling safe in the darkness and knowing he'd awaken instantly at any stealthy or unusual noise. But he was awake at dawn, chilled and stiff. He got to his feet, limped painfully to the fires and began replenishing them. Then he warmed himself beside one of them, waiting for Madrid and Daisy Elbert to awake.

When they did, they arose and all three ate some of the meat Daisy had cooked last night. Madrid brought in the horses and they saddled up. Dunbar stored the cooked meat in his and Madrid's saddlebags and tied what remained of the deer carcass, now black from exposure to the air, across the back of his saddle.

Even here, they could see their breath in the early morning air. Looking ahead, Dunbar could see the snow-covered peaks of the divide in the clear distance ahead of them.

He mounted stiffly and led out, favoring his leg more than yesterday. He was now sure it had festered because it was more painful than it had ever been before, but he didn't want to take the time to have Daisy rebandage it. Perhaps at one of the rest stops they took for the horses he could have her look at it.

Now, with every mile they traveled, the going became rougher. Brush on open slopes gave way to thick timber, and deadfalls barred their progress sometimes no matter which way they turned.

The trail became harder to follow since much of the time Morse rode on thick carpets of pine needles. Only Dunbar's practiced skill in tracking kept him from losing the trail.

At noon they stopped to rest the horses. Dunbar dismounted and began to unwind the bandage from his leg. It was difficult because there was only a slit in his pants and underwear but he was damned if he was going to take down his pants. Daisy came and knelt and took over from him, occasionally glancing worriedly at his face. He wondered if he looked as gray and cold as he felt.

The wound was festering all right. Dunbar got out his knife. He said, "Open it."

Daisy took the knife. She looked at his

face. "I can't."

Dunbar said, "Madrid."

Madrid took the knife from her. He knelt.

Pain seared through Dunbar's entire body. His head whirled and he felt himself falling through endless space. Then everything was black.

Chapter 19

Dunbar did not recover consciousness until early morning. His leg was one great area of pain, beside which his shoulder wound seemed trivial. His first thought was that he would not be able to travel because of the wound. He raised up slightly and felt gingerly of his leg, discovering that it had been rebandaged, apparently with the same bandages but in such a way that fresh cloth was over the wound each time the material was wrapped around his leg.

Surprisingly, despite the fact that his rest had been that of unconsciousness, he felt better than he had the night before. His head seemed clearer. He would ride, he told himself stubbornly, until Morse was caught and Luke rescued from him.

Light began to grow in the east. Madrid stirred and sat up and looked across at him. Dunbar noticed now for the first time that all three saddle blankets had been thrown over him. Madrid said, *"Buenos dias, señor. How are you this morning?"*

"Better. You two must be damn near froze."

"We had the fire, señor." Madrid got up, replenished the fires and stood with his back to one of them. Daisy awoke and sat bolt upright, her eyes wide and scared. When she saw Dunbar and Madrid, they calmed, and she got up and went, shivering, to stand beside Madrid. Looking at Dunbar she asked, "How does your leg feel now?"

"Better."

"Is it really better or are you just saying that?"

"It's better. It hurts, but it ain't the same kind of hurt it had in it yesterday."

Madrid left the fire and went after the horses. Daisy asked, "Do you want something to eat?"

Dunbar shook his head. He wanted water but he knew that would have to wait until they reached a stream. Licking his lips, he got painfully to his feet and limped back and forth between the two fires, loosening up the leg.

Both Daisy and Madrid ate some of the cooked venison. Madrid saddled up all three of the horses. He boosted Dunbar on his horse, then mounted his own. Daisy was already mounted, waiting. Dunbar led out again, still following the plain trail left by Morse.

At sunup they dropped down into a ravine where there was a small stream. Dunbar accepted help from Madrid in dismounting, then laid flat beside the stream and drank. After that, he splashed some water into his face and let Madrid help him once more onto his horse. Daisy watched the proceedings with worried eyes.

Dunbar rode out again. The trail climbed a timbered ridge, ran along a three-mile long saddle and began to climb again. The distant mountains, towering above timberline, were clearly visible this morning, though still more than fifty miles away. They could, perhaps, camp tonight in timber where the sweep of cold wind off the snowy peaks would be broken, but tomorrow they'd be up there exposed, and tomorrow night Morse would probably camp high above timberline and force them to do the same.

Furthermore, Dunbar knew that he himself couldn't last many more days. He was in constant pain and growing weaker all the time. The leg wound had festered once, and been opened and drained, but it would fester again and next time draining it might leave him too weak to mount and go on.

He also knew that in another day or two he was going to be too weak to face Morse even if they did catch up with him. Nor could he depend on Madrid. Madrid was willing to help but he wouldn't take the initiative.

Which left him with but one alternative. He must catch up with Morse before nightfall tomorrow or he would lose him for good. And he no longer had any illusions that Morse would release Luke alive. He'd kill Luke as easily as he'd step on a bug for no other reason than to get back at those pursuing him.

In midafternoon, Dunbar's head began to whirl. He steadied himself by holding onto the saddle horn until Daisy, directly behind him, said, "You're going to fall if we don't stop."

He turned his head. "Can't stop. Can't let him get that far ahead."

She didn't say anything and he understood the dilemma she was in. By insisting that he stop and rest, she diminished Luke's chances of being rescued alive. By failing to insist, she risked Dunbar's life or, at the very least, his ability to go on.

Dunbar could still follow Morse's trail even though his head felt light and his vision was sometimes blurred. He was a manhunter and following trail was a part of him.

But in addition to following trail, he kept his eyes on the high divide ahead. He had crossed it many times in the last six years from Canada to Mexico and he knew how important it was to cross where there was a natural pass. What he looked for this afternoon was the pass Morse would be heading for. Morse must have crossed the divide on his way to and from Denver many times. He probably knew exactly where it was easiest.

In late afternoon, after a particularly steep climb, Dunbar halted to give the horses a rest. Daisy brought some meat and handed it to him. "I know you don't feel well enough to eat, but try it. It will give you strength."

He took the meat from her numbly. It scared him the way he was weakening. He began to eat doggedly, without enjoyment but with stubborn determination. Daisy continued to eye him worriedly. He could see in her eyes that she knew the pain he was in, but she couldn't speak. She couldn't urge him either to rest or to go back.

On they went when the horses had rested for a while. Dunbar hadn't even tried to dismount, knowing how much doing so would have taxed his remaining strength. Going downhill was hardest for him. He had to brace himself with his hands against the saddle horn. Even so, the side-to-side motion of the horse was hard to endure.

But he thought he had spotted his mountain pass. Still twenty miles ahead, it was a notch between two high peaks. Out of the valley thus formed a stream grew, as evidenced by vegetation and a deepening cut as it descended from the peaks.

On either side of this notch which was probably a couple of thousand feet lower than any other visible part of the divide, bare and snow-covered peaks stretched away to north and south for as far as his eyes could see.

He studied it for the better part of the afternoon because he knew that upon his judgment and upon his being right depended Luke Elbert's life. The sun sank behind them, and the light faded from the sky. Dunbar guessed that by the time darkness forced a stop, they were five miles from the pass.

He had already decided what he was going to do. Going on this way, following Morse and Luke, gave all the advantages to Morse. He had the boy as a hostage and as long as he did he knew his pursuers dared not attack.

Dunbar wasn't sure he had the strength. But he intended to go on, tonight, after the others had gone to sleep. He intended to try and get ahead of Morse, and ambush him when he came past. The trail told him Morse was no more than a couple of hours ahead. It was certain he wouldn't try to cross the pass tonight. It was doubtful if he'd camp in the cold above timberline. Dunbar figured he could circle, and get ahead.

He slid from his horse, nearly falling as he did. He collapsed to the ground and closed his eyes. Madrid would take care of his horse. Daisy and Madrid would gather wood, build a fire and cook more of the venison. They might even find, here, a trickle of water or at least some snow to eat.

Daisy came and knelt beside him and put

her hand on his forehead. She said, "You're feverish."

"I'll be all right," he mumbled. She started to get up and he said, "Daisy?"

"Yes?"

"I want you to wake me when you and Madrid turn in."

"Why?"

"Maybe I'll feel like eating then. I don't right now and I know if I don't eat I'll be weaker tomorrow than I am right now."

She said, "I'll wake you."

"Do you promise?"

She looked strangely at him but she said, "I promise."

He let his eyes close, then, and let himself drift away into a dreamless sleep. When Daisy touched his shoulder and gently shook him awake he was sure he could not have slept more than two or three minutes at most. But the fires had died to a bed of coals and the stars were bright in the sky.

Madrid had gathered a large quantity of pine boughs, some of which had been put over him in addition to the saddle blankets. He forced himself to get up and hobbled to the fire. Daisy gave him some venison, hot from being spitted over the fire. He ate it and accepted some snow she had found in some sheltered spot. He didn't want to eat, but it was the pretext upon which he had persuaded her to awaken him and he knew he must.

Eating, he listened for the horses and located the place where Madrid had picketed them. Without seeming to, he searched the perimeter of the camp until he located his saddle, and bridle.

Madrid brought more wood and replenished the fires. Dunbar finished eating, ate a little more snow, then returned to his bed and laid down again. His rifle was beside him, his revolver still in its holster at his side. Daisy asked, "Do you want me to take off your boots?"

"Huh uh. They'll be all right."

She put three saddle blankets over him and he did not protest because he knew it would do no good. But he didn't close his eyes. He didn't dare. He laid there and stared up at the stars until he heard Madrid begin to snore softly.

He shifted his position and watched Daisy carefully to see if she would move. She did not. He came carefully and silently to a sitting position. Still Daisy didn't move.

Carefully, painfully, Dunbar eased himself to his feet, using his rifle for support. Daisy turned over and sighed, but she did not awake.

Pain made Dunbar dizzy. He didn't know if he could manage this but he knew he must. Carrying his saddle blanket, he hobbled painfully to where his saddle was. He tried to lift it and failed. Half carrying it, half dragging it, he went to where his horse was picketed. He put the bridle on, threw on the saddle blanket and then, with a supreme effort, heaved the saddle up.

He rested then, leaning against the horse to keep from falling down. After a few minutes, he forced himself to secure and tighten the saddle cinch. Having done that, he shoved the rifle into the boot, walked to where the picket pin was driven and pulled it out. He coiled the picket rope, slipped it off the horse's neck, then hung it from the saddle horn.

He rested now, again. At last he knew if he didn't get into the saddle soon he never would. Hanging onto the saddle horn with both hands, he forced his left leg up and into the stirrup. Again using mainly his arms to lift himself, he swung up into the saddle.

He didn't hit it sitting down, but sprawled face downward across the horse. The animal danced a little, but didn't buck or run.

Dunbar righted himself. He reined the horse away from camp, maintaining a slow, careful walk so as not to awaken either Daisy or Madrid.

At last, a quarter mile from camp, he let the horse move out into a brisk walk. He realized that he was gripping the saddle horn as if his life depended upon not letting go.

His head whirled and all he wanted to do was fall off the horse and close his eyes. It took an enormous effort of will to look ahead, to fix his eyes upon the distant notch that marked the mountain pass.

He reined a little to the right so that he would not pass too close to Morse's camp, wherever that might be.

Occasionally his leg brushed against a tree. When it did, bright spots would dance before his eyes. He had never felt such pain and hoped he never would again.

Up, up he went, though not continuously. There were ravines, rocky and difficult, that had to be crossed. There were deadfalls that had to be detoured. But at last he came to the edge of the timber and could look ahead, could see the notch toward which he was heading.

He need not worry, now, about where Morse was camped. A stiff, icy wind blew down toward him from the high divide and he knew Morse would not have camped where he was exposed to such a wind. He put his horse up the steep, bare slope.

Occasionally a patch of snow left over from the winter past, would bar his way. Several times he let the horse plow through. Twice he went around, since the snow looked deep enough to bog down the horse.

At last he reached the crest of the divide. He had hoped there might be high rocks from which he could leap down upon Morse or at least shoot down at him but there were not. There were only a few scattered rocks, big enough to hide a man but not a horse and the land was almost flat.

Accordingly, Dunbar rode the horse on down the other side until he found a place where he would be out of sight. He tied him to a rock, then withdrew his rifle from the boot and hobbled back to the summit of the pass.

The wind whistled through the rocks. At this altitude it was like ice and it chilled him immediately.

He eased himself down behind the biggest of the rocks. He laid his rifle down beside him and pushed his hands under his armpits to keep them warm.

Hunched there, shivering, in pain and thoroughly miserable, he waited for the dawn.

Chapter 20

Before dawn began to gray the sky, Dunbar knew he would be helpless when Morse did ride through the pass unless he somehow kept himself warm. He got up, and flailed his body with his arms. Though his thigh wound was causing him extreme pain, he forced himself to hobble back and forth, trying to restore circulation to his legs. He kept this up for a full half hour, and at last began to feel a slight warmth in his skin as blood began to circulate again.

A line of gray outlined the horizon in the east. From his own travel pattern, built up over the years, he knew that Morse would probably be riding as soon as it was light enough to see. When that time came, he would have to be hidden and would have to stay hidden until Morse rode into sight.

He kept flailing himself with his arms and pacing back and forth for as long as he dared. Then he crouched down again behind the rock, sheltered partially from the wind and hidden from the trail leading up to the pass over which Morse would have to ride.

He began to worry now. What if he miscalculated Morse's route? What if Morse did not come this way at all? Morse was capable of planning just such a deception and then going another way.

And even if Morse did come this way, how could he shoot the man without endangering Luke? He had no answer for this question, and he could have no plan. He couldn't know what he would do until the time for it actually came. But if he made a mistake, and injured Luke or killed him, or if he caused Morse to kill the boy, then Daisy would be forever lost to him. That was the chance he knew he took.

With increasing light, the wind picked up velocity. It gathered snow from the unmelted patches and swirled it across the barren mountaintops, reducing visibility to less than three hundred yards. Though the increased wind further chilled him, Dunbar welcomed it. Morse would be closer to him before he became visible. Reduced visibility gave him the slight advantage of surprise.

But it also created another problem. Morse might pass him beyond the range of his visibility, to right or left, and go by without his even knowing it.

Sourly he cursed himself for having so many doubts. He had planned as well as he could. He had committed himself to the course he thought offered the best chance of rescuing Luke. If he failed he failed. There was no way of guaranteeing himself success.

With that decided in his mind, he gave his attention to the trail leading up toward him from below. But his mind kept wandering. He wondered if Madrid and Daisy had awakened yet. He wondered what they had thought when they found him gone. Madrid would find his trail, and they'd follow it, but Morse's fate, and Luke's, would be decided long before they could arrive, no matter how hard they rode.

Faintly, he thought he heard a sound. He held his breath, listening. The wind howled even more vengefully than before and he cursed it silently because it kept him from hearing a repetition of the sound.

But suddenly he heard it again, and knew unmistakably what it was. It was the ring of an iron-shod hoof on barren rock. A horse was coming up the trail.

Dunbar felt weak with relief. This wasn't over yet, but at least he had been right when he had guessed that Morse would come this way. Furthermore, judging from the direction from which the sound had come, he knew Morse was coming straight at him and would not pass outside his range of visibility.

He slid his hands from beneath his armpits where he had been holding them to keep them warm. He picked up his rifle, shocked at how bitterly cold the receiver was. A cartridge was already in the chamber. He eased the hammer back to full cock and half raised the weapon, waiting until the approaching horse would become visible through the blowing snow.

But deep inside him he knew he didn't have much chance. If Luke was in front of Morse, he wouldn't dare to shoot. If Luke was behind the man, he'd be afraid of the bullet going through Morse and killing Luke anyway.

A shadow took shape in the driving snow. A horse, a man . . . And then Dunbar was able to see Luke. The boy was in front of Morse. One of Morse's arms was holding him. The other held the reins.

Warm, unhurt, and with something to steady his rifle on, Dunbar might have risked a shot at Morse's head. The way things were, he didn't dare. He was so cold that he was numb. He was so weak, his hands holding the rifle shook. He was beat. He'd have to let Morse ride on by. Unless, by threatening to kill both the boy and Morse, he could force Morse to drop Luke in exchange for the promise that he would be allowed to go his way.

Steadily, head down, Morse's horse plodded up the slope. Tail and mane bannered out in the bitter wind. Luke was hunched down, his face nearly buried in the hollow of his shoulder. Morse had a blanket wrapped around him against the cold and the corners of it whipped in the wind with sounds like pistol shots.

Dunbar considered shouting at Morse, and telling him to stop. He decided against it because it would only alert the man. No. What he did would have to be done without warning or there would be no chance whatever of success.

He raised his rifle, his numb and nearly

frozen finger on the trigger. He couldn't feel the trigger and so kept the pressure slight for fear of discharging the weapon accidentally. He sighted on Morse, then lowered his point of aim to the horse's near hindquarter. It wasn't as big a target as he would have liked but it was the best he was going to get.

When the bullet struck, the horse would undoubtedly jump unless the bullet shattered the bone in his leg. When he jumped, Dunbar would have to pray he threw both Morse and the boy. And while they were separated on the ground, he would have his chance at Morse. He'd have just one chance and that was all. If he missed, Morse would seize the boy and use him as a shield, and Dunbar would have lost.

Morse was now only fifty yards away. It was a miracle he had not already seen Dunbar crouching there. Only the driving snow and bitter wind had prevented it. Dunbar knew he dared wait no longer. He tightened his finger on the trigger as gradually as he could.

The report was strangely flat and faint here at the peak of the world and the wind snatched it away, leaving a silence broken only by the eerie howl of the wind and the pelting of snow granules against Dunbar's clothes. For the barest instant there was no perceptible reaction on the part of either the horse Morse was riding or the man himself.

Then the horse sagged. His hindquarter gave way and he seemed almost to sit on the barren, rocky ground.

Morse, taken completely by surprise, did not seem, at first, to realize the horse had been shot. Perhaps the noise of the wind had drowned out the almost slight sound of the report, in itself so swiftly snatched away by the wind.

Morse stepped off the horse as the animal went down, still holding onto Luke. The horse began struggling, trying to get up but unable to.

Luke saw Dunbar first. Morse himself was preoccupied with the horse. Luke kicked at Morse, and struggled free, and for the barest instant, Dunbar had his chance to shoot.

He seemed to be moving with elaborate slowness as he jacked another cartridge into the gun and raised it to his shoulder to sight it on Morse's chest. Before he could pull the trigger, Morse saw him, and seized the boy. With his free hand, he grabbed for the revolver in its holster at his side.

But he was as cold as Dunbar was, his extremities just as stiff. His hand closed over his gun grips but he could not seem to drag the weapon from its holster. Perhaps it was frozen to the holster and stuck there or perhaps there simply was no strength in Morse's numbed and nearly frozen hand. Dunbar croaked, "Drop him! Damn you, let him go!"

Luke kicked savagely, but his back was against Morse, the outlaw's arm encircling him and there was no force in his kicks. And Dunbar dared not shoot.

Frantically he yelled, "Luke! Get away from him!"

Cold as he was, numbed too, Luke literally exploded into a flurry of action. His head dropped and he sank his teeth into the arm holding him. At the same time he twisted his body and his hands went up to claw at Morse's eyes.

With a savage curse that Dunbar didn't even hear because the wind snatched the words away, Morse let go of him. This time, Luke wasted no time. He plunged away from Morse, traveling nearly ten yards before his numbed legs gave out and dumped him to the ground. Even then, he didn't stop, but crawled frantically.

Dunbar at last had his chance. This time he was ready, with rifle raised and cocked.

He got his bead as Morse turned and started after the boy.

Dunbar followed him the way he'd have followed a flying duck and fired and for an instant thought with horror that he had missed. Then, like the horse, Morse went almost slowly and deliberately to the ground. But he didn't stop trying to reach young Luke because he knew that only by using the boy as a shield did he have any chance at all.

Dunbar fired again, and this time missed. He fired a third time and must have hit again because Morse stopped moving toward the boy. Luke had made it to his feet and was stumbling away.

Morse turned to face Dunbar, dragging at his stuck revolver again. Dunbar approached him, rifle ready this time, and cocked. As Morse got his revolver suddenly free of its holster and raised it, Dunbar lifted the rifle to his shoulder and sighted it. Morse's revolver came up, and from a distance of less than ten feet the bore looked enormous.

Both guns fired simultaneously, but as Dunbar's rifle discharged, he was already falling. He had put his weight too suddenly and too carelessly on his wounded leg and it had simply given out, letting him fall sideways and sprawl to the snow-covered ground.

Morse's bullet struck the rocks behind Dunbar and ricocheted off into space with a high, diminishing whine. Dunbar's bullet, coming from a rifle pointed at the sky when it discharged, was lost in the blowing snow.

The two men were now almost close enough to touch. Dunbar scrambled toward Morse, hoping to hit him with the rifle, but he saw he wasn't going to have the time. Already Morse was once more bringing his revolver to bear.

Dunbar fired instinctively. He saw the tiny hole appear in Morse's forehead and knew it was over at last. Morse was dead. He would move no more, was no longer any threat.

He let the rifle fall from his hands. He struggled to his feet. The blanket Morse had been wearing was blowing across the ground.

He reached it, stepped on a corner to stop its progress, then knelt to pick it up. He shouted, "Luke!"

The boy, running awkwardly, turned, catching his voice clearly because he was downwind. His glance went from Dunbar to Morse's body lying on the ground and then back to Dunbar again. Suddenly Luke began running, straight toward Dunbar as fast as his legs could carry him.

Dunbar dropped to his knees and caught the boy who struck him with enough force to almost knock him down. Luke's body was shaking and sobs came wrenched from him as if by some inner force. His arms went around Dunbar's neck as if he was never going to let go again.

Dunbar's own arms tightened on the boy and he held him close until the boy's agony had eased. Luke wiped his cheeks and nose on the shoulder of Dunbar's jacket. Dunbar wrapped the blanket around him, got up, and limped to the wounded horse. He shot the animal in the head, then hobbled to where he had left his own animal. He led him back to where Luke sat huddled in the blanket on the ground.

He didn't know how he was going to mount. He only knew he must. He put his good foot in the stirrup, supporting his weight by holding to the saddle horn. He said, "Boost, Luke. I ain't going to make it by myself."

Luke was up in an instant, boosting with all his strength. Dunbar sprawled face down across the saddle, and fought to get his leg over and bring himself upright.

Having done so, he reached down and

took the blanket from Luke's hands. He put down a hand and hoisted the boy up, settling him in the saddle in front of him. He turned the horse back in the direction from which they had come, leaving Morse and his horse lying there, already beginning to freeze in the icy wind, knowing they might not be found until next spring.

The cold was still a numbness in him, and pain was constant and terrible. But Luke felt warm against him and with the protection of the blanket, he knew they'd make it to Daisy and Madrid.

And the anticipation of seeing her, of seeing her face when she first glimpsed the two of them put a warmth in him that was better than any physical warmth could ever be.

The publishers hope that this Large
Print Book has brought you pleasurable
reading. Each title is designed to make
the text as easy to see as possible.
G. K. Hall Large Print Books are
available from your library and
your local bookstore. Or you can
receive information on upcoming
and current Large Print Books
and order directly from the
publisher. Just send your name
and address to:

G. K. Hall & Co.
70 Lincoln Street
Boston, Mass. 02111

or call, toll-free:

1-800-343-2806

A note on the text
Large Print edition designed by
Bernadette Strickland.
Composed in 18 pt English Times
on an Editwriter 7700
by Debra Nelson of G. K. Hall Corp.